Chantel's Song

Gwen Hulbert

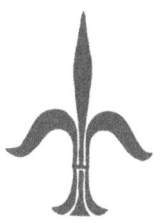

Copyright 2021

The Christward Ministry
First Edition

All rights reserved. No part of this book may be reproduced without written permission except for quotations embodied in critical articles or reviews. For additional information, write to:

The Christward Ministry
20560 Questhaven Rd.
San Marcos, CA 92078

questhaven.org
questhavenacademy.com

A publication of The Christward Ministry

ISBN: 978-1-7374607-0-1

In loving memory of Gwen Hulbert
whose love for the spiritual journey and the art of writing
come together in this book to make something beautiful
for God and all who read it.

Contents

Introduction	7
Chapter 1 - Preparation for Birth	9
Chapter 2 - Chantel's Welcome	15
Chapter 3 - Billy the Kid	23
Chapter 4 - Carol Ellen's Shining Friends	33
Chapter 5 - Teen Testings/Lessons	39
Chapter 6 - Sounds of Music	51
Chapter 7 - Becoming William	69
Chapter 8 - Nature's Inspiration	75
Chapter 9 - They Meet Again	81
Chapter 10 - Deeper Sharing	89
Chapter 11 - Out of the Past	95
Chapter 12 - Meeting the Family	107
Chapter 13 - Upward Path	117
Chapter 14 - The Wedding	127
Chapter 15 - Ideals, Dreams, Openings	141
Chapter 16 - Ideals Become Reality	155
Chapter 17 - Middle Years at the Sanctuary	173
Chapter 18 - Full Circle	183

Introduction

Drawing upon the invaluable lifetime lessons she received from her gifted spiritual teacher, Christian Mystic Flower A. Newhouse, Gwen assumes the role of storyteller using the power of story to give readers a tiny glimpse into how human lives evolve lifetime after lifetime from before birth to after death. Touching on the importance of each choice we make and how we respond to each challenge placed into our lives to help us grow spiritually, readers gain an understanding of the lessons we each come to earth to learn and how meeting those lessons from a place of love empowers our upward growth. From where we now stand in our journey through life, we may, with Gwen's help through this book, discover valuable insights into how we might enhance our own return back to God.

CHANTEL'S SONG

Chapter 1
Preparation for Birth

She had just gotten back from a wonderful session of music—Beethoven this time, with subtle nuances of glorious new harmonies—when Chantel was called. At first the merest bubble of golden tone, it soon resonated within her entire being. A thrill of excitement ran through her—the time was near!

At last, she understood why it would be necessary to return to earth—how needful it was to work out the unfinished karma that kept her from total freedom. The music still filling her, she began inwardly to prepare for this *most important* interview. Friends had told her that it would probably be coming soon.

Then shortly they themselves disappeared into the dense lower world to act on and apply what they had learned here in the higher worlds. Tomaro, Sarita, Kerrie, and finally her dearest friend William had all passed over the threshold into the dense world. She had been at their graduation celebrations; they had shared laughter and tears till their very moment of entry into the earth.

As the curtain of heavy mist covered her friends, she could no longer see them nor even feel them. Although she missed them terribly, she was happy at their chance to be given the opportunity to correct past mistakes, improve tangled relationships and bring new insights to the world.

She remembered William gently stroking a pure white Akita puppy as he vowed to bring through the new modes of healing that he'd learned here. "I must try, and with God's help I will succeed!" Another time, while watching Chantel weave beautiful music textures and colors in the atmosphere around them, he had asked, "Will you join me in this work, Chantel? You can hear the anguish of those in need. You're discovering the power of music to inspire and to heal. I've learned sensitivity of touch, and how the energies of light can be used to purify, recharge, and heal lives. The world deeply needs this synthesis to bless those who are ill in body or mind."

She had not been able to give William a definite answer just then, not sure yet what direction her life would take. She recalled vividly her last conversation with him: "Dear William, you have a worthy goal, and I wish you the highest good. It may be that someday we'll have the privilege of working together. But there are still so many lessons we both must learn, and many remnants of unfinished debts we owe others. Only when those are cleared will we be free to effectively perform a healing work. Let us resolve to first help each other with life's lessons, then in time the greater work may follow. All blessings to you, dearest friend!" Then his Call had come, and with it his preparation for reentry into the denser worlds.

Now that she had received her Call, Chantel once again reviewed what she had learned of the proper way to meet the great Presence, the Kindel Angel. She knew that it was necessary to come to complete stillness, to be open and expectant. This way she could come to attunement, receptive to the best possible guidance from her highest self as well as from the accrued experience and wisdom of this great Archangel.

There would be a combination of reverence and respect for the Angel, as well as a sharpening of her own qualities of intuition. Together, then, prayerfully, they would be able to plan just the right life for Chantel in the dense physical world.

Earlier, she'd experienced a review of her life and had been shown clearly where she'd made mistakes and wrong choices, as well as observing the solid steps of growth she'd accomplished. Chantel had pondered deeply the reasons behind her relationships on earth, and the paths that her life had taken. She resolved, "This time I will willingly take on the challenges that will enable me to make steady, firm steps upward in evolution. Just give me the chance to prove myself."

As Chantel responded in thought to the Call, she was instantly in the Presence of the great Kindel Archangel. He looked at her with eyes that penetrated her entire being. He understood her fully. There could be no secrets, no concealed motivations. All her past, her present, and her potential were open to Him. His gaze into and through Chantel was intense, yet totally accepting, and filled with a great impersonal love.

Then He conveyed, with full communication that made words unnecessary, the following:

"My child, you have been called so that together we can plan your life in the physical world. In the higher spheres you have discovered, explored, and been taught much. Returning to earth will give you the opportunity to apply what you have learned. It will not be easy, as you will not have the clear sight and understanding that are found here. But it is *only* on earth that you can work through your unfinished karma and make rapid progress in evolution. It is *only* on earth that you will be challenged, tested, yet put in circumstances that will allow your fullest potential to bloom."

The Archangel then presented Chantel with an array of choices, ranging from the country of her birth, to her parents and siblings, her friends, career, talents and weaknesses, her body type and state of health, even her astrological sign. With an occasional impression of, "You would do well to overcome this negative trait" or "This friend will be of great help to you," or "You will learn much from this experience," together they decided on a plan for Chantel's upcoming incarnation. For each of the choices, lessons could be learned, relationships developed, talents cultivated, or testings overcome. The Kindel Angel then created a disc from pure energy, placed within it the living symbols that had been fashioned for Chantel's pattern, and set it spinning toward her heart area. This life graph would remain within her aura throughout her new physical incarnation.

Shortly after, Chantel entered a semi-sleeping "twilight state." This period prior to birth in the world helped her to rest, to be calm and serene regarding the earth life she was about to enter. At the time of conception, she felt a flash of joy and love from her parents-to-be. Other than that, she rested and waited while her physical form grew ever more complex and detailed. Occasionally she would be drowsily aware of music, singing, gentle laughter, or loving murmurs. But mostly, she slept—warm, protected, and sheltered.

Chantel's Song

Chapter 2
Chantel's Welcome

Pressure, gentle at first, rhythmic but insistent, woke her. "I want to sleep. What's happening?" More pressure, harder. "No, I'm not ready yet. Let me sleep some more." More waves of constriction, propulsion, heaviness. She opened her eyes to darkness. "What happened to the beautiful colors, the music, the gentle billows of light? Please, no more squeezing. I'm afraid—let me go home!"

The Angel of Birth gently soothed and calmed Chantel in her infant body still in the womb. She said, "Do you remember when the Kindel Angel planned your life to come in the dense world? Do you remember what you were going to accomplish, the brave words you used? Here is your first opportunity to prove both your courage and your compassion. If you do choose to return to the Shining Homeland, as you certainly may, you will only postpone the time of your growing and your learning experiences in the dense world. But more important, your decision will bring great sorrow and loss to your parents. They will not understand that you are truly alive; they will feel guilt. They will grieve for your "death." Your mother will feel that she has done something wrong. Your father will also feel a great aching emptiness and will be sad that he can't give his wife happiness.

"They have tried for years to have a baby. Their home is prepared; they are so looking forward to your arrival! Remember the music you heard in your dreams? That was your mother singing to you. Remember the deep rumbling sound you liked so much? That was your father laughing joyfully as he talked to you. Remember the pounding noise that would make you stir a bit? That was your father converting the spare room into your nursery and putting together the furniture for your room. That freshly redecorated room and the empty crib would remind them of your absence in their life."

"But this hurts! What if I can't make it? I'm so afraid."

"Open yourself to them; try to sense their love for you."

Slowly, slowly, she became aware of warmth. Gradually she began to see color too, as pink as the heart of a rosebud. As she forgot about herself, focusing her attention more on the pink warmth, she saw its shape and source. The pink glow was beaming from two individual sources and formed a heart shape that focused directly on her. She relaxed, immersed now in its gentle warmth, as the glow continued to grow.

"Where love is, there is no room for fear."

With a countenance of indescribable beauty and majesty, the Angel of Birth urged Chantel across the threshold.

"It is time—come now and bring them joy!"

Chantel reached out, drawn inexorably to the physical, yet gazing steadily into the eyes of the Angel of Birth. From the Angel's heart came another ray of love, then the light radiating from Her being became unbearably bright. Then there was nothing but the Angel's face—pure light, pure love.

❦ ❦ ❦

It was a difficult delivery. Sara had gone into labor a week late. After 14 hours of contractions, and a dose of Pitocin, things were nevertheless at a standstill. Sara was exhausted. The doctor, equally tired after 24 hours on call, told Sara and Tom. "We'll have to start prepping for a C-section. Both mother and child are getting too worn out."

"Please, Doctor MacIntyre—if there's any other options—no C-section. Two of my friends died of complications from Caesareans. The thought of having one frightens me a lot."

Tom, meanwhile, had turned gray at the mention of a C-section. "Isn't there anything else to do, Doctor?"

"Well, we'll give it another hour, but we can't let either Sara or the baby be endangered. Try to rest as much as you can, both of you, between contractions."

"All right, we'll try," Sara replied. The doctor left briefly to answer a page.

Sara and Tom held hands tightly, both frightened

but each trying to reassure the other. Sara whispered a prayer from her heart. "Dear God, please help us. We have been awaiting this dear incoming soul for so long. I ask your peace and your strength for this delivery, so that the little one will have a good healthy beginning to this life. Especially may the gateway be opened and the way be eased for him or her. God, if you will, send your Angels to keep our little one healthy. Thank you."

"Amen," echoed Tom.

Unseen by Sara or Tom, a healing Angel entered the room and stood at the head of the bed. She briefly greeted Her superior, the Archangel of Birth, with a warm outpouring from her heart chakra. She then ministered to the mother, sending gently flowing waves of renewal and relaxation throughout Sara's aura. After a moment she placed light hands on Sara's forehead and cheeks, encircling her with love. Sara sighed, smiling, and dropped off into a light sleep.

Gliding to the side now, the Angel concentrated on the baby. Her hands above Sara's abdomen moved in healing, energizing patterns, producing streams of light that would penetrate and invigorate the new infant body.

While doing this, she simultaneously sent a strong direct mental flash to the attending nurse. "Check the IV now!"

To the nurse, whose aura brightened momentarily, it seemed a mere nudge from her own subconscious— "I've checked everything over and over, but just maybe I should look at the IV one more time." Then she stepped over to the tubing, and saw that it had become pinched. After freeing it, she sent up a quick "Thank you" to whoever or whatever had urged her to recheck the line.

The Healing Angel had nearly completed her Light work in this room. Briefly she turned to Tom and quickly, lightly, placed two fingers near the center of his forehead. Ripples of soothing calmness permeated his aura. When Sara awoke later, he told her that all at once he "just knew that things would be all right."

This particular Angel had as her area of service the obstetrical section of the hospital. In addition to her primary caring for mothers-to-be, she radiated her beams to the rest of the family present in this wing of the hospital. With a last swirl of healing and reassurance, she passed through the wall to the next person in need.

Her work was accomplished both directly and indirectly. If necessary, she would nudge the baby into a better position for birth. Often, however, her work involved inspiring the attending staff of physicians and nurses to *individualize* the most appropriate treatment for each patient. Most of the staff couldn't see her of course, but the nurses in particular were likely to notice the difference in atmosphere when this Angel was present. To others her inspiration came across just as "hunches," or perhaps a sudden "aha!" idea.

A large part of the Angel's work involved clearing the area of fear. Most often the recipients were unaware of the work being done for them. However, once in a while a patient would feel a gentle touch as of loving hands, or warmth to an area being healed. She might say something like, "I don't know why, but I'm not afraid anymore."

While the great Archangel, the Angel of Birth, prepared the soul for the ceremony of transition into this infant body, the healing Angel worked on amplifying currents of peace, calmness, and strength to the new form. This was in addition to the healing beams that were directed to the mother to course through her body and renew her energies.

At this moment that Sara felt another great wave of pain, yet of strength to endure, the Angel of Birth said strongly, "Come Now!" One mighty push, and the baby was here.

※ ※ ※

The last thing Chantel saw with her inner vision was the loving, ever-brightening luminosity of the Angel of Birth. The light became so brilliant that she had to avert her gaze. Her body was still in the dark place; constricted, heavy, with inexorable rhythmic pressure squeezing her. There was ever more pressure—then a sudden emergence into harsh lights and coldness.

A whack, a startled gasp, a howl. Then the rumble of a deep voice: "Congratulations, Sara and Tom! You have a baby girl."

With gentle but firm hands, the nurses checked her thoroughly, measured and bathed her, then wrapped her in warm blankets. Nestled in the blankets, she was placed in Sara's arms. Here she felt love, warmth, and security. She knew then that everything would be all right as long as her mother's arms were around her.

Tom was overwhelmed with a mixture of emotions. His face mirrored his exhaustion, pride, gratitude, and love. His voice choking, he babbled, "It's a miracle! She's so perfect. I love you—oh Dear God, how I love you both!" And then a few minutes later. "Are you sure you're all right? Are you sure she's all right?"

"Yes darling, we're both fine—tired but incredibly happy—and we love you very much." Sara continued, "Do you remember the affirmation we used to say to welcome our new baby? Now that she's here we can recite it with even deeper meaning."

He nodded, clasped his wife's hand, and tenderly stroked their baby nestled in the blanket. Then together Tom and Sara half-whispered:

Lift the veils, O Spirit of Life
That the Incoming One may feel
Our earnestness and welcome.
As earthly parent, I vow to Thee, Eternal Parent,
To bless, sustain, and love this child, patiently.
I pledge myself to fulfill the duties of parenthood
With enduring remembrance and vision.

Chapter 3
BILLY THE KID

Billy was a scrawny nine-year old, not a boy you'd normally notice. He was maybe a little smaller, a little paler, and a little scruffier looking than the other kids. He'd long since learned that the way to get by was to blend into the background.

His teachers paid little attention to him, having to spend much of their energy on the troublemakers: what was left went to the rare gifted student who needed challenges to keep mentally stimulated. Billy fit neither of these categories. To all intents and purposes, he was invisible.

On this Friday afternoon he meandered toward home after school, kicking a pebble with his scuffed tennies. There was no point in hurrying. Ma would just shush him the minute he came in. Billy's father had abandoned them when Billy was about two years old, and now there was a succession of "Uncles" that would move in for a while and then disappear.

After working two jobs, his mother was always too tired to pay much attention to Billy. About the only thing she'd said to him in the last three months was, "Quiet—don't wake up your 'Uncle.'"

He greeted his classmate Harry at the next corner. "Hey man, what's up?"

"Some of us are gonna go over to the old Caslan place. You wanna come along? Might be somethin' cool over there."

"Sure—just let me dump my books—I'll meet you here in half an hour."

He made it home and was halfway down the hall before Ma called absentmindedly the familiar "That you, Billy? Quiet, your "Uncle" is sleeping."

Billy kept on going, dropping off his books on the kitchen table. He gulped some milk from the carton in the refrigerator and then let himself out the back door. Billy's old hound lay in the dusty yard under the shade of a rusty pickup. He heaved himself up when he heard Billy coming. Billy scratched him on the head and poured more water for him. "You're a good dog, Hooshee. I'll be back pretty soon."

With a sigh, the dog settled back into the shade. In his younger days he would have come along wherever Billy was headed, but now resting and sleeping were about all he could manage.

Billy smiled, remembering how the hound had come to be called "Hooshee." About three years before, late one night during a bitterly cold rainstorm, Billy was awakened by a voice softly calling his name.) At first he'd thought he was dreaming, but when he pinched himself to check, it hurt. That made him decide that he had to be awake. Three times he heard, "Billee—Billee—Billee." It sounded as if the mystery voice was coming from the tree outside his bedroom, but no matter how hard he looked, he couldn't see anything but the rain.

He knew for sure it wasn't his Ma; as far as he knew, nobody in the neighborhood had a voice that gentle and sweet. Could it be old Mrs. Stuart next door? No way! She was snoring so loud he could hear her through his open window.

Very, very quietly, so as not to wake anybody, Billy answered. "I'm here. What do you want?"

The voice said, "Go downstairs and look on the porch. He needs you. Take good care of him, Billy."

So Billy tiptoed downstairs, carefully stepping over the two "giveaway boards" that creaked when he ran down fast. He heard a rustling—it sounded for all the world like a whirlwind in the yard. The deadbolt was stubborn as always, but he finally got it to move, and yanked the door open. Just outside lay a shivering, drenched, skinny dog. He wagged his tail feebly and then was still again. Billy ran to get a blanket, accidentally making enough racket to wake up his mother.

She threw on a bathrobe and half-stumbled to the doorway while yelling at Billy. "Just what do you think you're doing? You're supposed to be in bed!"

"Ma, look. He's so tired, so thin, and he's freezing. We've got to help him!"

"That mutt! How did you know he was there?"

"A voice called me—it said to go look on the porch, and to take good care of him."

"That's ridiculous—you were dreaming!"

"But Ma, he's here now, and he needs to get warm! We can't leave him out on a night like this!"

Billy stooped to pet the dog. All at once he saw a bright beam, almost as though someone was aiming a flashlight directly on the two of them. He'd never seen a flashlight beam like that though—it was golden and felt warm and comforting somehow. As soon as it shone on the dog, he stopped shivering and thumped his tail once more.

Billy lifted his eyes to see where the light was coming from. For an instant he saw, shining in the brightness above, what looked like a tall, slim, long-haired lady with huge, beautiful eyes. Then she and the light were both gone. "Ma! Who's she?"

His mother yawned, "OK, Billy, I guess he can stay for a while, and if you want to call him "Hooshee," well, why not? But you've got to take care of him, because I sure don't have the time."

"No, Ma—I mean, who's she? She was standing right out there, shining the light on the dog."

"Light? What light? What in the world are you talking about? There's nobody around here except you and me." She yawned again, hugely. "Well, if you're going to take him inside, go on and do it, but mind you don't let him on the bed. Remember, you're gonna take care of him. I'm going back to bed so's I can go to work in the morning."

"Good night, Ma. Don't worry, he'll be good."

"He'd better be—otherwise you've got to get rid of him."

Billy brought the bedraggled animal into the kitchen, rubbed him dry with towels, then fed him some warm milk and a slice of leftover meat loaf. Afterward, the two of them headed up the stairs to Billy's room. The dog instantly settled down to sleep on the rag rug by the foot of the bed, but Billy lay awake for a long time trying to figure out the voice, the golden light and the shining whoever-it-was out by the tree. Just before he finally dropped off to sleep, he heard the same gentle voice say,

"Thank you."

Now, three years later, as Billy was patting Hooshee, he thought again about the mysterious light and the stranger with the beautiful voice. How come his mother hadn't seen them? They'd been clear as day.

As he headed off to meet Harry, he wondered what the guys were planning. The Caslan house had been empty for a couple of years now, ever since Mrs. Caslan got sick and had to move into an old folk's home. It had always been a pretty scary place anyway, with dark thick trees and bushes looming around the house.

Harry and his friends Ted and Sam were taking turns throwing knives at a tree on the corner. Behind them, thumbs in their jeans, slouched a couple of eighth-graders, Ralph and Walt. Harry acknowledged him with a, "Hey Billy."

The two older boys whispered to each other, nodded, and then sauntered over to Billy. Looking him up and down, Ralph said, "You're sure skinny. How old are you, kid?"

"I'm nine, and I may be skinny, but I'm strong."

A long pause, then another nod, "We're going to check out the Caslan place. If you want to tag along with us, you've gotta keep your mouth shut. Can you do that?"

"Sure, but what are you gonna do?"

"Didn't I say to keep your mouth shut? You'll find out when we get there."

With that, the boys set off. Billy tried to recall what he'd heard about the house and the folks that used to live there. Mrs. Jones at the library had said that long ago it had been the center of social events for the town. She also said it was classic Victorian architecture, whatever that was. All Billy could remember was a big wooden two-story house with lots of windows and funny trim around the roof and windows. Its white paint was peeling so much it reminded him of his worn-out scruffy tennies.

A long time ago he'd seen a wrinkled, white-haired lady working inside the garden in front of the Caslan house. Hobbling around with a walker and wincing in pain with every step, she was trying to prune the roses out front. He'd watched her for a while, noticing how hard she struggled with that job. He still remembered her amazingly sweet smile as she finished each bush, and how she'd reached out a hand and touched it lovingly, seemingly murmuring something to it.

Soon the boys arrived at the decrepit place. Ringed with dark, dense evergreens, it had a heavy and sad look. Beyond the wrought-iron fence, they could see the lawn area gone to dry patches of weeds, with broken bottles and trash all around. Ralph checked carefully to make sure nobody else was nearby watching. He shook the padlocked gate, then started giving orders in a harsh whisper.

"O.K. Harry, you're going over first—Sam, throw your jacket on top of the fence so he won't poke himself on those sharp tips. Go around the whole house. Check for any open windows or doors. If you find a way in, whistle three times. If not, sneak back through those bushes over there. Ted, boost him up—now! Me and Walt will stand watch for you guys."

"You can't just break in like that—that's not right!" exclaimed Billy.

"Hey runt, I told ya to keep your mouth shut—so just shut up and stay out of the way!"

Hunching deeper into his shabby jacket, Billy backed off to sit under a huge fir tree that overshadowed the gate. He watched as his friend climbed over the wrought iron stakes and dropped lightly to the ground inside. Harry dashed up the walkway to the front porch and rang the front doorbell. When there was no answer after a minute, he ducked into the bushes nearest the house, headed to the first window, and tried to open it. He continued furtively all around the house—behind the bushes—to the window—behind the bushes—to the door, and finally reappeared alongside the front porch. He raced back to the gate, gasping, "Can't find anything open. Around to the right's the kitchen. The screen's busted and one of the boards in the door is loose. Maybe somebody real skinny could squeeze through."

Ralph scowled at the boys clustered around him. "Nah—you guys are all too fat. Where's that little kid who was just here?"

Sam pointed over to the sheltering fir tree by the gate. "Hey you—get over here!"

Reluctantly, Billy got up and came closer to the group.

"C'mon, hurry up. Harry's found a way in. All you have to do is go through that side entrance and then unlock the front door. We'll meet you there. Go on, do it!"

"What are you gonna do inside?" asked Billy once again.

"What's the matter—you scared?" sneered Ralph. "What a baby!"

Before Billy could respond, Walt spoke. "It'll be O.K., kid. I'll boost you up. We just want to look around."

With that he interlaced his hands to help Billy over the fence. Billy dropped down inside next to Harry. The two of them raced from bush to bush, finally reaching the door with the loose board. As they began to tug at it, Billy whispered, "I don't think we should be doing this."

Harry whispered back. "Don't worry; nobody will

know. Just think how much neat stuff must be in there." Then he sneaked back to the front door to join the others.

With one last creak, the board gave way. Billy squirmed through, finding himself in a darkened room filled with heavy old-fashioned furniture. In one corner was an ancient upright piano. He couldn't resist hitting a few chords. The out-of-tune instrument protested, its strings echoing eerily in the room.

Stirring up clouds of dust with every step, and hardly able to see in the dimness, Billy eventually found his way to the front hall. As his hands fumbled at the door lock to let the others in, he clearly heard a kindly but very firm voice clearly saying, "Billy, stop! Don't do this!"

He gasped, spun around to see who had spoken to him—but no one was there. At once he knew with certainty that what he had been about to do was completely wrong. This voice, somehow associated with the house itself, was startling, but not frightening. Billy felt as though the voice had just set him straight, giving him the courage to keep from making a big mistake.

Suddenly he heard Hooshee howling piteously outside by the loose board. Billy dashed back through the parlor and squeezed out through the opening while the dog was scrabbling desperately through nails and broken glass to get to him. "Hooshee, what is it, boy? How did you get here?" The dog was panting from the exertion; his paws were bleeding from his struggles to reach Billy. A gentle, sweet, and oddly familiar voice directed, "Take Hooshee home—now. He needs your help." Billy saw a golden warm light surrounding the dog. Instantly he remembered when he'd heard that voice and seen that light before—three years ago when he first found Hooshee. This time, though, he saw no one.

Hooshee led the way out. After limping painfully across

the side yard under a huge overhanging weeping willow, he managed to wriggle through a concealed hole under the fence. Then he quit howling and collapsed in exhaustion, unable to walk further. Billy dug away at the hole with his hands, making it big enough for him to push his way under the fence, scooped up the dog, and raced down the alleyway toward home.

Meanwhile, at the Caslan place, the other boys had heard creaking steps, spooky ghostly music, and a horrible long wailing, howling noise. What sounded like footsteps again was followed by lots of scuffling and rustling dragging sounds. The place was haunted, that's for sure!

Wide-eyed with fear, they fled back over the front fence. A sudden wind blasted leaves, trash and dust from the yard straight at them. The house creaked ominously, and branches whipped noisily about in the gusts.

A police car drove by slowly, then turned around and stopped. By this time, the kids were terrified. They all started running down the sidewalk.

"Hold it right there!"

Looks like a tornado's comin' up. You boys better get yourselves home right away."

Ralph responded: "Y-y-yes sir. We're on our way."

Then they scattered, racing to beat the threatening weather. None of the boys even thought about what might have happened to Billy.

Nobody was home when he got back, so there were no questions to answer, thankfully. Billy had seen the tornado clouds too, and knew how important it was to get to the cellar quickly. He stopped only to grab a towel and a bucket of water. Once they were safely in the cellar, he took care of Hooshee's wounds and comforted him while they waited for the "all clear" to sound. After they got back upstairs, Billy finally cleaned himself up and swept the hall to get rid of the muddy leaves that had dropped on the floor when they came home earlier.

Billy spent the next few nights pondering the events of the day and giving thanks for having been protected from doing something very wrong.

For the next few weeks, the faithful dog slept on the rug by Billy's bed, just as he had on that stormy night when he first came to the house. Billy talked to Hooshee as though the dog was his best friend. Night after night he wondered what had really happened at the Caslan place that day. Although he couldn't fully understand, he knew it was very special. Billy always ended with a "thank you" to that *someone* or *something* that had kept him from making a huge mistake.

Chapter 4
CAROL ELLEN'S SHINING FRIENDS

Carol Ellen, her shoulder-length blond hair bouncing and blue eyes sparkling, dashed back to the first-grade classroom after lunch. It was Wednesday afternoon—her favorite school period, because of "Music Hour." Most of the time, school was OK, even though it would be much more fun to be playing with her special friends in the back yard—Shana, her green companion in the willow tree, and funny little Griff by the rock wall.

On Wednesday afternoons though, school was always wonderful. Her teacher, Mrs. Aliano, would have the students listen to music. Sometimes she would explain what the music meant, other times all the kids got to tell stories about what they thought it was saying, or how it made them feel. Afterwards Mrs. Aliano would bring different instruments so they could hear what kind of sounds those made.

Today she brought in a harp and played it. Carol Ellen loved this music and told the class it sounded like angels playing in a waterfall. The kids laughed at her for saying that, but then the teacher showed Carol Ellen how to hold her fingers on the harp and make the sound of the waterfall too. She was thrilled. Still strumming the harp, she looked at Mrs. Aliano, and beside her she saw a shining Angel singing along with the harp notes. Carol Ellen's eyes got huge, and she burst into a wonderful smile. Then she blinked and the Angel was gone.

Mrs. Aliano saw Carol Ellen's big eyes and radiant smile and heard her whispered *thank you*. Thinking this was for her, the teacher smiled back. "You're welcome, dear. It does sound lovely, doesn't it?"

Carol Ellen already knew that most grownups couldn't see her special friends and thought she was just making up stories. They might use big words like "active imagination," or "fantasizing," but she'd learned that was just another way of saying that they didn't believe her. So now she didn't even try to explain to her teacher what she'd seen. That story would just have to wait till she got home. She could tell Mommy, and then share with Shana and Griff.

The warm happy feeling from the Angel's song stayed inside her all the rest of the day. When she got home, she dropped off her jacket and book, then found her mother, who made a point of being home when Carol Ellen was due back from school.

"Mommy—guess what! Mrs. Aliano let me play the harp today. When I was playing I saw an Angel. And I heard her too."

"Sweetheart, that's wonderful. Will you tell me about it?"

"She was bright, with colors round her that kept

changing with every note she sang. It was as if the colors were sounds, too. She had the prettiest voice I've ever heard. But when I blinked I couldn't see her anymore. Just thinking about her now makes me feel really happy."

"Carol Ellen, what a special day this has been for you. I'm so glad you told me!"

"Mommy, what do you suppose she was? A Harp-Angel?"

Her mother responded: "From what you just told me, it must have been an Angel of Music that you saw. Their whole life is given to joyously serving God through singing. People who can see them say that the colors in their auras are ever-changing, and that they make beautiful thought-forms out of the music's energies. Do you think she put a thought-form in your aura—one that's making you feel so good?"

"I bet that's it! Oh, the harp is such fun to play! I hope Mrs. Aliano lets us try it again. Waterfall music is my favorite."

"I'm happy that you had such a nice time with the music, honey. Go on outside and play now while it's still light. Remember to stay in the yard."

"O.K., Mommy—see you later," she called, as she headed out the back door. Once in her yard, she skipped over to a smooth-barked sycamore and gave the tree a hug. Then, hooking one hand around the trunk, she spun round and round it until she was dizzy. She giggled, switched hands, and then spun again in the other direction. Finally, she plopped onto the grass, while the leaves, sky and clouds whirled around her in gradually smaller arcs.

After things settled down, Carol Ellen began talking softly, not only to herself, but to the tree as well, just as though it could hear and understand her. Remembering the magic of "Music Hour," she murmured, "It was a wonderful sound, you know. Have you ever heard a harp?"

To her delight, a breeze came up, fluttering the leaves and branches of the tree and making light arpeggios. "Uh huh, it sounded a lot like that," she chuckled, and heard a tiny joyous laugh in return. A rainbow-colored "something" flashed in the air but zipped out of sight before she could get a real good look at it. So often she'd been aware of these little shining beings but could never bring them into clear focus. They seemed to be made of shimmer and sheen, and always made her smile.

That was funny, because her eyes were fine—things like flowers or butterflies were sharp and crisp—even hummingbirds with their whirring wings had a shape she could see clearly. But these happy little companions were always just a flash of brightness, and then went away. She used to tell her friends at school what she was seeing, but they made fun of her and said she was being silly, so after a while she stopped telling them about these sparkling, joyful playmates.

Her mother, though, always listened with full attention and never laughed at her. Carol Ellen remembered how her mother had once asked, "Sweetie, can you tell me more about these little shimmering beings that you see?"

"Well, some are as tiny as a bumblebee, others are about as big as my hand. They sparkle with lots of colors, mainly the colors of the flowers they're near. It looks as if they're always moving, darting really fast. There's some in the sky too, every time there's a breeze. They dance and do somersaults in the wind. When they laugh, it sounds like tiny bells tinkling, and the sound makes me happy deep inside." As Carol Ellen described them, she realized again with puzzlement that not even her dear mother could see these tiny "shimmerers," as she called them.

Soon she picked herself up from the grass and headed toward the willow tree and the old stone wall to tell Griff and Shana about seeing and hearing the Angel of Music and getting to play the harp. They were both delighted to hear about Carol Ellen's special experience. Griff smiled broadly and Shana hugged her. Carol Ellen then wondered aloud why nobody else in class had seen the Angel, and why even her mom couldn't see the shimmerers in their garden.

Her nature companions explained that when humans are born, they have what's called "inner vision," but as they get older, most of them lose this. Griff said, "It's like they get thick and stuck—all covered in mud so they can't see or hear us anymore. Poor humans!"

Shana added, "Most of them don't even remember—so much beauty and life all around them, and they haven't any idea that it's there. Do you know, Carol Ellen, most people think *we're* not real? They say we're just part of fairy tales, and they forget all about us as they grow up."

"That's the silliest thing I've ever heard! How could anybody think you're not real?" After a moment, Carol Ellen solemnly promised them, "No matter what,

I'll remember you both forever and ever."

　　Just then, her mother called her to dinner. Carol Ellen dashed off to the house, repeating in a whisper, "…forever and ever."

Chapter 5
Teen Testings / Lessons

Mister Marsh, the U.S. history teacher, droned on, reading an apparently endless string of names, dates and events in an unvarying monotone. For a few minutes, Billy tried to take notes, but soon gave it up as a lost cause. As usual, he hadn't gotten enough sleep the night before. Now he sat in the back row of the classroom, struggling to stay awake during this last class of the day. He stretched out his legs, inadvertently nudging someone's foot. Unfortunately, this was Joe, a guy who had been bullying him mercilessly ever since he first started high school.

"Hey—wadda ya think you're doin? You just kicked me!"

"It was an accident–OK?"

Joe wasn't about to let it drop. "You got no business poking into my space, man!"

Nearby, the other kids began stirring—some life in

the class at last! Their comments began as whispers but became progressively louder...

"Hey, what's going on...did he diss you?... Who's that...what'd he do?...he kicked him...I didn't see nuthin....don't let him do that to you...kick him back!"

As the noise grew, Mr. Marsh glared over his glasses, focusing on the source of the disturbance. Slamming the textbook on his desk, he strode to the back row. "Both of you—out! Report to the principal's office right now!"

As they headed to Mr. Phelps' office, Joe hissed nonstop threats and insults at Billy. When they arrived, the principal asked with a sigh: "Well, boys, what is it this time?"

"He kicked me!"

"No, I didn't—he had his foot stuck out!"

"Did not!"

"Did so!"

The principal cut short the exchange with, "OK— hold it! One at a time. Billy, you first."

Billy cleared his throat. "Well, we were sitting in Mr. Marsh's class and I stretched my legs because they were going to sleep. Joe's foot was in the aisle, and..."

Joe interrupted, "You kicked me on purpose with those big ugly shoes of yours. Look here—you scuffed my Nikes. Can't you even get decent shoes, man?"

Billy flushed, acutely aware of his big generic tennies, bought two sizes too large so he'd grow into them. Since his mother abandoned him a few years back, he'd been living in a foster home, where it was made very clear that they couldn't spend money on "frills."

Both boys then burst into explanations, each trying to justify his own side. The principal listened to the squabbling a few minutes, then held up his hand, with a brief "Enough!"

Having himself taken Mr. Marsh's history class when he was younger, he well remembered the dull recitations that used to bore him nearly to sleep. He didn't doubt that Billy was having a rough time staying awake, or that Joe was eager for any distraction. He considered briefly, silently asking for guidance in dealing with ways to handle the situation. Joe had a long-standing reputation as a troublemaker and Billy was the quiet kid that often got picked on. Nevertheless, Phelps didn't think they hated each other specifically: he felt this was typical adolescent behavior for them.

After a moment, the answer came: have them work together on a hands-on project. At least they'd get some practical experience, and maybe they'd learn to understand each other better. Tom Altmer, in Maintenance, had a real knack for dealing with kids; teaching them a work ethic and helping them develop practical skills. Many students who had been heading toward delinquency got turned around by Tom. Maybe it was his patience, maybe it was his gift of listening to find out what they really hoped to do in their lives, maybe—who knows—he was an angel in disguise.

While Billy and Joe stood awkwardly in front of his desk, gazing at the floor, the principal picked up the phone and punched in a number. "Tom—Phelps here. Listen, I've got two tenth-graders in my office that need some shaping up. How about taking them on for a couple of weeks? …Good—they'll be there in 20 minutes. Thanks!"

Mr. Phelps turned back to the boys. "Both of you, look at me," he commanded. "Now!"

As they did, he gave them a piercing gaze before continuing. "I want you to stay here till the bell rings; then go talk to Mr. Marsh. Tell him I've suspended you from his class for two weeks. You've got to keep up with all his classwork while you're out, so be sure to ask him for the next assignment. Then get yourselves over to Mr. Altmer in Maintenance, on the double. You'll be working for him right after school—two hours a day till the end of the month. Understood?"

Billy answered quickly, "Yes, sir!"

Joe threw Billy a withering glance before acknowledging the Principal with a reluctant "Yeah."

"Go sit over there—quietly!—while you're waiting," the principal said, indicating a couple of stiff chairs along the wall.

They sat. Joe glared at Billy, then furtively began to jab him between the ribs with a sharp pencil. When Billy gasped, causing Mr. Phelps to look up, Joe would put on his most innocent face. After an interminable 15 minutes, the bell rang and the boys dashed back to their history classroom. Joe threatened, "I'll get you for this. Just you wait, you little runt!"

The other students had left immediately, leaving Mr. Marsh fussing with his papers on the desk. He looked up over his glasses with a quizzical, "Well?"

Joe and Billy repeated what Principal Phelps had told them about the suspension, then asked for their assignments.

"Two weeks, hmm? You'll have to read chapters seven through ten, and then write a 500-word paper on the most important influences on that era. That's due the day you get back, at the beginning of the period. Also, be prepared for a test the day after that."

After another long pause: "That's all; you're dismissed."

Next, remembering Mr. Phelps' "on the double," they sprinted to the Maintenance building. As before, Joe spent the entire time cursing and insulting Billy. The building was a metal shed that smelled of oil, hot metal, paint and cleaning fluids. Peering in the open doorway, the boys were surprised to see the array of machinery and equipment housed there. Although the shed was crowded, it looked neatly organized and spotlessly clean.

Tom Altmer looked up from the lawnmower he was repairing, saw the boys at the door and beckoned them inside. He stood up, wiping off his hands with a clean rag, as he slowly looked them over. After a moment, he nodded slightly and asked their names. Joe, looking at his feet, muttered almost inaudibly.

Mr. Altmer wasn't about to let that go. "Joe, is it? Look at me, Joe, and stand up straight. It's important to always speak clearly when you're introduced; people shouldn't have to strain to hear your name. I'm glad you're here." He then stuck out his hand. With obvious reluctance, Joe took his own hand out of his pocket and exchanged an extremely brief handshake.

Then Altmer turned to Billy with, "What's your name, son?"

43

Billy straightened up and shook the proffered hand, with a slightly louder, "Um, I'm Billy."

Mr. Altmer looked directly into Billy's eyes, greeting him with, "Welcome, Billy. It's good to have you here." Billy was surprised, but nodded—the man radiated trust and honesty.

"OK, boys, today you'll be digging holes on the hill behind the football field. We need to plant some trees there for a windbreak. You'll see blue flags where the trees should go. Holes have to be at least one foot deep and three feet wide.

"Gloves are in the second drawer to the right; grab yourself a pair. Shovels and picks are on the wall. I'll be out to check the job in a while."

Billy and Joe got their equipment and headed out, Joe grousing all the way. "That stupid guy thinks he can order me around. Who does he think he is anyhow, making me do his work? I'll show him!" Billy remained quiet, trying to sense what it was about Mr. Altmer that made him different.

Soon the boys arrived at the hill. Joe halfheartedly turned over a spadeful of earth, hit a rock, and swore. Ignoring the flags now, he found a spot where the soil was saturated with moisture. "No point in killing myself on this crummy job. This is where I'm gonna dig. You go find your own place."

Billy had already located a flagged site in much harder material near the top of the hill. As he wielded the pickaxe, it seemed to him that trees would certainly be needed there. He worked steadily to make a hole the required size.

The hole Joe dug was finished much sooner because of the soft, wet soil there. After a while, Joe strolled up the hill with his spade full of muddy dirt, throwing it onto Billy's back while he was bent over trying to take out a big rock.

Furious, Billy spun around, but Joe had already moved out of range, sarcastically saying, "Oops—the shovel must have slipped!" With a malevolent grin, he added, "Doesn't make any difference though. Your clothes were dirty to begin with, just like your filthy shoes."

Billy responded, "Shut up, Joe—you're asking for it!" as he closed in on Joe.

"Go ahead, hit me," sneered Joe. "I can't wait to tell Altmer that you started this!" After that he lazed on the grass, mocking Billy. "Hey wimp, can't you even dig a hole? What a baby!"

Seething inside, but knowing that Joe was just looking for a fight, Billy managed to keep his silence and not react to Joe's baiting. He worked doggedly till Mr. Altmer appeared when the task was done. Altmer looked at the results, sighed, and beckoned them, saying, "C'mon on back, boys—time to clean up."

Once they got back to the metal building, the groundskeeper pointed out the equipment cleanup area. Joe slammed his tools on the floor, flung down his gloves, and stormed out. "Forget it, man, I ain't gonna do no more stinkin scutwork!"

Billy wavered uncertainly. In a way he wanted leave too, in order to get the approval of his peers, but another part of him was trying to understand what Mr. Altmer would do about Joe's rebellion.

Altmer responded calmly: "Let him go, Billy. He'll learn eventually. Leave his stuff where it is and clean up your gear."

Billy whacked the dirt off his gloves outside, then came back in and rinsed the shovel and pickaxe in the huge sink. The older man pointed out some rusted areas and showed Billy how to remove them with a steel wool pad. Next he had Billy grab a clean rag to dry the tools, finally coating them with lightweight oil to keep them in good shape.

He then commented, "Good job—just hang them up on the back wall across from the window. Remember, if you take good care of your tools, they'll work well for you when you need them."

When that was done, he said, "That's all for now, but here's your assignment for tonight. I want you to think about what a tree needs in order to grow and thrive. See you tomorrow."

The boys showed up at Mr. Altmer's shop the following day. Joe's tools had been moved to a corner but were otherwise as dirt-encrusted as he'd left them. Altmer indicated Joe should use those, then issued Billy a freshly sharpened shovel and brand-new gloves.

Joe stomped off, cussing all the while. On reaching the hillside, he threw the tools aside and walked off campus, with "I've got better stuff to do than hang around here with a loser, digging stupid holes."

Billy began digging diligently. Even though he was getting more sore and sweaty by the minute, Billy nevertheless was feeling good about getting the job accomplished. Mr. Altmer had been unobtrusively watching them the whole time, and now strolled out from the shed.

He gazed out in the direction that Joe had left, murmured something about some people having to learn things the hard way, then turned to Billy. "Take a break, son. Tell me, have you figured out what a tree needs yet?"

Billy replied, "Well, I s'pose it needs water and sunshine, lots of dirt, and some sort of fertilizer."

"That's a good start—what else do you imagine a tree would need to make it a really great tree?"

Billy contemplated that for a while, then slowly responded, "I guess the dirt can't be too soft and wet or the roots will get weak and it'll topple ... it needs to reach up to the sky so the leaves can get the sunlight" He paused a long time, finally adding softly," I think it might need friends too."

"Why do you say that?"

"Well, it would get lonely all by itself. It needs birds and squirrels to share its space. I really think they could help each other, don't you?"

Mr. Altmer smiled slightly, saying simply, "Billy, you're starting to learn about trees, and about life. Once you're done, come on in and we'll get these tools cleaned up."

※※※

Joe finished barely half of the assigned two weeks, dragging his feet all the while. He'd show up late, insult Billy, and do as little work as possible. Much of his energy was spent cursing and fuming at the unfairness of "the stupid system." When Mr. Altmer made suggestions that would improve his work techniques, he'd roll his eyes in disgust, insolently ignoring the advice.

After that, Joe never went to class again. The next day, and several days following, he'd show up across the street from the school, taunting Billy and trying to goad him into responding. When nobody else was around to watch, he'd throw empty beer cans at Billy, saying, "You must be thirsty: here's a drink." And, "You look like you're cold: this'll warm you up," as he threw cigarette butts and matches onto the dry grass where he was working. Later, when Joe encountered Billy in town, he would sneer and make belittling remarks like "Are you still sucking up to the janitor? Unplugged any good toilets lately?"

Billy continued his sessions with Mr. Altmer, doing whatever was asked of him. One day while they were cleaning the tools, Mr. Altmer asked, "Don't your parents worry when you're late from school?"

Billy flushed. Reluctantly he admitted, "I never knew my dad, and Mom left town with her boyfriend a while back, so I'm in a foster home. As long as I'm not a bother, they pretty much don't care."

Altmer's response was simply: "I understand: I was a foster kid too."

After his two weeks of assigned duties were up, Billy continued to work with Mr. Altmer after school, having developed a real liking for this activity. While learning more practical skills in landscaping and repairs, he also made a little money to buy new clothes and some school supplies. Under Mr. Altmer's tutelage, he also learned how to diagnose and repair motors, do basic carpentry and woodworking, keep inventory, select materials wisely, and keep equipment in good shape.

His foster family barely noticed that he was gone for a few more hours each day. They weren't mean people, just totally absorbed in their own problems. Billy wondered how he'd be able to stay out of their way when school was over. The answer came when Mr. Altmer asked Billy if he would like to help out part-time during the summer. His foster mom readily signed the consent form, with an off-handed "that should keep you from getting bored."

As time went on, Billy developed a respect for Mr. Altmer that he'd never had for anyone before. This quiet, wise, nonjudgmental man taught him by example as well as with words. Moreover, Billy could talk to him and not get put down or ignored. For the first time in Billy's life, someone truly listened to him. Billy ended up spending the rest of high school apprenticing under Mr. Altmer when classes were over. In addition to a strong work ethic, he learned all sorts of practical skills, from carpentry to plumbing to electrical repair. The timorous, apathetic Billy who'd had to serve two weeks of detention was being transformed into a new person. Manual labor made him strong and fit, and successful completion of tasks gave him confidence.

Billy not only listened carefully to Mr. Altmer's advice, but even more importantly, observed his behavior. He didn't just talk a good thing—he *lived* it no matter who he was with or what he was doing. For the first time in his life, Billy had a trustworthy, inspirational father figure.

From this mentorship, Billy gradually found his own strong moral compass.

Chapter 6
SOUNDS OF MUSIC

Auditions had been called for 3 o'clock in the school theater. The two dozen kids waiting to try out for *Sound of Music* were chattering in small groups, occasionally bursting into laughter at private jokes or the antics of the class clown. Several were bragging that they'd get the lead, or at the very least a major part. One of the girls pulled out a mirror and began redoing her hair to show it off to best advantage. Another, wearing leotard and tights, was working on stretches, totally aware that most of the guys were staring at her attractive and fully displayed figure. The room was dominated by confident extroverts.

The conversation stopped once the three teachers who would be doing the judging entered the auditorium and seated themselves in the front row. In a commanding voice, the drama and speech coach addressed the students.

"These tryouts will be in alphabetical order, so

please line yourselves up that way at the back of the stage. We expect respectful silence throughout this audition. When you're done, come down here and take a seat. Do not leave until all of you have had your turn. I would suggest you keep your eyes and ears open so you can listen and learn from the others."

He then listed the factors that would be considered—voice, projection, movement, and interaction—and explained that each of these would be evaluated on a scale of 1 to 5. He concluded with examples of what was most important to him. Next, the music teacher and dance teacher each briefly described their own specific emphasis.

Taking over again, the coach added, "This audition is not to try out for a specific part, but to give us an idea of your overall abilities. The three of us will tally the results and come to a decision.

"You'll each be assigned one minute of dialogue, one minute of music, and one minute of movement." He gestured to center stage: "We've asked Tracy, a theater major from the college, to read and interact with you, play the piano for your song, and direct you in a simple dance sequence."

Tracy flashed a smile at the students, saying, "Hi. Looking forward to this."

The coach concluded, "Final casting will be posted by the main stage door on Friday morning. Any questions? If not, let's begin.

"Achana? Gloria Achana? Step up, please. Tracy—give Miss Achana her sheet." With that, the audition was underway.

Chantel was almost always prompt and would have been at the audition in plenty of time. However, on her way over, one of the smallest freshman girls had slipped and twisted her ankle in the hall just a few feet in front of her. Chantel quickly helped the youngster to her feet, picked up the books that had fallen out of her backpack, then half-carried, half-walked her over to the nurse's office.

By the time Chantel made it to the theater, Glenn Storrs was on stage, loudly projecting his lines. Glancing at the few students left backstage compared with the many in the seats, she surmised it might be too late. After watching for a moment, she turned to go, frankly relieved that she wouldn't have to audition. This hadn't been her idea, after all. Her voice teacher was the one who'd insisted that she try out for the musical, asserting that it would be a valuable experience and would improve her confidence in front of a group.

Before she got fully offstage, Chantel heard the speech coach calling her name: "Wyler? Chantel Wyler?"

With a slight sigh, she answered, "Yes sir, I'm here."

"I need you right up front, right away. Take your lines from Tracy and let's get going. We're almost out of time."

Chantel scanned the lines. Startled, she realized they resonated with her beliefs and feelings. She found herself speaking them with conviction and sincerity, as though they came from her own heart. The song selection was equally appropriate: her clear sweet voice, which was often rather soft, carried to the far corners of the auditorium. Since she'd had no training in drama or dance, the movement and interaction part of the audition was not polished, but she had an innate grace that carried her through that portion too.

As soon as the audition ended, she dashed back to the nurse's office to check on the freshman who had fallen. The nurse was taping her ankle, while at the same time instructing the girl on proper care and treatment of the injury.

"Feeling better by now?" asked Chantel. "Do you need help with your books?"

"Thanks, I'm OK. My mom's going to pick me up in a little while. That was awfully nice of you to get me here to see the nurse." Sticking out her hand, she added with a spunky grin, "My name's Brenda."

"And I'm Chantel," taking the proffered hand with a smile. After a moment, Chantel said, "OK then, take care—see you around."

Chantel went to pick up her purse and books, then remembered she'd left them in the auditorium. She raced back, hoping to get there before the doors were locked. Luckily, it was still open. There were a few people in the room, discussing the auditions. She went in, grabbed her stuff and was heading out the back door when she heard her name.

"Hey, did you hear that last girl, Chantel something or other, singing?"

"Yeah, she's a real nobody, but she absolutely blew the judges away—you could tell by their expressions. I'm sure she'll get a part."

"With that voice, it'll probably be a big one."

Not waiting to hear any more, Chantel shook her

head in disbelief. All she'd done was sing and read some lines—what was so special about that? The audition hadn't been as scary as she'd thought it would be, but it was good to be done with it. She would tell her voice teacher that she'd tried out; that would be the end of it.

By Friday she'd put the experience totally out of her mind. Between first and second period, she was surprised when a couple of students congratulated her.

"For what?" she replied.

"Well, duh—as if you didn't know."

"Actually, I don't," she said, mystified.

"Then you'd better get yourself over to the stage door to check it out."

She headed over to the auditorium, wondering, "Do you suppose they want me to do voiceover singing for one of the cast, or maybe student coaching for the songs? That would be fun."

Arriving at the door, she read the cast assignments for the play. To her astonishment, she had been cast as Maria. The Captain's role was given to the most popular boy in school. As she scanned the list, she realized that everyone else was popular and outgoing. All the parts were filled except for Gretl, the youngest daughter.

Chantel's mind flashed back to little Brenda, the youngster she'd helped a few days ago. "Hmm, bet she'd be great for that. She's certainly small enough, and has no problem expressing herself."

After rehearsal, Chantel asked the drama coach if he'd consider a freshman for the role.

"Well, it's always been seniors with sometimes a

few juniors thrown in, but there's nothing in the rules that says we can't cast anybody as long as they're good actors. Who've you got in mind?"

"Sir, this is the smallest student in school, but she's cute and seems outgoing and confident. I imagine her voice would project quite well. Her name's Brenda."

"Well, why not? Go ahead and ask her; if she's interested, have her come see me."

The next day, Chantel made a point of seeking out Brenda near her locker. "Hi Brenda—how're things going?"

"Just great, thanks. My ankle was just sprained; they taped it and it hardly hurts at all now."

"That's terrific." After a pause she continued, "This may sound strange, but would you be interested in trying out for the part of Gretl in *Sound of Music*? That part hasn't been cast yet."

Brenda's stared at her in amazement. "What? You're kidding, right?"

"Absolutely not."

Brenda squealed: "Oh my gosh, how did you know that *Sound of Music* is my very favorite play in the whole world? All my life I've dreamed of being in it."

"Then go see the drama coach right away. I can't promise, but he did say it would be OK to drop by."

"Oh wow! I can't believe this!"

The following day, the coach took Chantel aside and thanked her for sending Brenda: "I think she'll be perfect for the part."

Rehearsals were proceeding well, and Chantel gradually became more comfortable with the rest of the cast and crew. Their values were quite different from hers—all of them were hugely impressed by glamour and fame, the juiciest gossip and the latest styles. They had enormous egos. Their world revolved around themselves. Nevertheless, most of them soon accepted her as part of the cast. "She doesn't talk much offstage, but she's OK."

The day before dress rehearsal, the boy cast as Captain von Trapp showed up even later than usual. Act one was already underway. Cocky but charming, he was generally able to talk his way out of trouble.

He entered with his standard boisterous announcement—"I'm here. Did you miss me?" A couple of minutes later, he sidled up to Chantel who was in the middle of a scene with the von Trapp children, and whispered, "Hi, beautiful—did *you* miss me?"

She shushed him. "Dave, you're not in this scene—you know you shouldn't be onstage now."

"Playing hard to get, eh? That makes you even more irresistible. Can't wait till Act Two so we can make beautiful music together."

As the characters playing the von Trapp children began to snicker at this outrageous interruption to the scene, the drama coach broke in with, "Maria, don't break character, and Captain, get off the stage right now! What were you thinking of, anyway?"

"Must have just got carried away." He sauntered offstage, chucking little Brenda under the chin and giving her a wink as he left. She blushed bright red, both embarrassed and flattered at this attention from the good-looking senior.

The rehearsal continued with no further incidents but lasted longer than normal. Chantel was concerned about getting home before dark. As soon as it was over, she rushed to grab her books and purse, then ran off the school grounds as fast as she could. Dave noticed her hurry, checked out which direction she was going, and decided to follow in his freshly polished sleek new car. He figured that after a couple of blocks she'd be glad to get a lift wherever she was going. Then he thought, "Why not wait for her to run four blocks? That way she'll be tired and be really grateful to get a ride with me. Besides, who wouldn't want a ride in this hot car?"

So he did just that, cruising behind slowly enough to keep track of her, but not close enough for her to see him in case she turned around. After the full four blocks, he drove up a bit ahead of her and parked alongside the road.

With a big show of surprise, he said, "Hey Chantel, what's up? I'll give you a lift—hop on in."

"No thanks, Dave, I'm fine."

"C'mon, Chantel, don't you trust me?"

"It's not a matter of trust, it's just that rehearsals ran late, and I've got to get home right away."

"Well then, you'll get there quicker if I drive you, and we can get to know each other better on the way. It's a win-win, right?"

"Sorry, that won't work. Bye." And she took off running again.

Too stunned to even turn on the ignition, Dave just sat there with his hands on the wheel. "What just happened? Nobody's ever turned me down before. What's with this girl—I was trying to be nice to her, offer her a ride in my car, and she refuses?"

He sat in the car for a long time, going from bewilderment, to anger, to soul-searching. Their conversation kept running through his mind. Finally, he drove home, continuing to mull over that experience through the evening. That night he had a dream where he saw the scene reenacted, but rather than being in it, he was an objective bystander. He watched the actions of the obnoxious, bragging, arrogant, kid in the car with revulsion. Shocked into wakefulness, he realized that was himself!

Chantel had already sized up Dave—good-looking and talented, but self-centered, spoiled, and with a huge ego. Underneath it all, though, he was not a bad guy. Jogging home, she chuckled at his bravado and his disbelieving response to her turn-down.

She got home, tousled and breathless, and went straight to the kitchen for a quick bite. Thank goodness, she'd made it before Dad got home. He was very protective of her, and if she wasn't there by the time he got home from work, he'd start phoning her friends. If they didn't know where she was, he'd start driving around looking for her.

Her mother came in from the back yard where she'd been working in the garden. "There you are, Chantel. What kept you?"

"Rehearsals ran late, Mom. The bus had already left so I walked home. A guy in the play offered me a ride, but it didn't feel right. You should have seen the look on his face when I turned him down—like he'd never been rejected before! He's popular, and a good actor, but really stuck on himself."

Her mother smiled understandingly. "It's good that you listened to your intuition." Opening the refrigerator and pouring each of them a glass of iced tea, she continued, "If he's a good person underneath, he'll grow from the experience."

As they sipped their tea, Chantel murmured, "Still, he is really good-looking, and his car is practically new. Oh well—he'll probably never speak to me again."

"I'm not sure about that—you may have piqued his interest. Or is it the other way around?"

"Maybe just a little bit," she admitted.

They sat quietly for a while before getting up, Chantel to do her homework and her mother to fix dinner. They parted with a hug: "Thanks, Mom, for always being so understanding. Love you lots."

At rehearsals the next day, Dave played his character with a conviction he'd never shown before. Gazing intently at her, the Captain interacted with Maria as though truly living his role. After the rehearsal, Dave sought out Chantel, who was getting her things together to leave.

"Can we talk?" he asked hesitantly.

This was totally unlike the Dave she'd seen for the past several weeks. There was no bravado, no banter, just a polite boy asking her if they could talk. Mystified, she responded, "What about?"

"I just want to apologize for coming on so strong yesterday. I was a jerk. If you'll forgive me, I really would like to drive you home this afternoon."

Cautious, she paused a moment, listening to her intuition. When she sensed that he was sincere and it would be all right to spend some time with him, she told him, "OK—just let me call Mom and tell her we're coming. That'll give her time to fix some snacks for us."

"Sure—I'll be ready whenever you are."

After she finished phoning, they walked over to his car together. "Where to, Maria—Innsbruck, Vienna, the mountains??" he teased.

"Well, Captain von Trapp, this time let's just go to Oakcrest Place instead. It's a lot closer."

In the car, he quickly regained his confidence. They talked about the play, teachers, and school in general. He told her that as soon as he graduated, he was planning to head to Hollywood to work in the movie industry. His ultimate goal was acting, but he had enough film production skills to be useful, figuring he'd do that to survive in Hollywood till "the big break." He concluded with, "I've got connections. I'll be on screen before you know it."

Chantel responded that she hoped to continue singing but wasn't sure what direction to take. Her plan was to go to the college where her mother had gone, majoring in music. With a solid liberal arts background, she'd have far more choices as to her ultimate profession.

"Four years is a long time—do you really want to wait that long to start your career?", Chantel asked.

"Definitely! The school has great teachers; this will be a chance to keep getting first-class training. There're so many choices and so much still to learn! It's going to be fun to find out what I love best and get really good at it.

"Still sounds like a waste of time. Me, I know exactly what I want to do. I've got the talent, I've got the connections, and nothing's gonna stop...!"

Before he could finish, Chantel interrupted, "Turn right at the next corner. Our house is the third one on the left."

Dave pulled into the driveway with a flourish. "Look—I need to make a good impression on your mother. How can I get on her good side?"

"Don't worry about anything—just be yourself."

They entered the house, following the scent of cookies baking. Sara hugged her daughter, then smiled at Dave when Chantel introduced them. "Let's sit right here in the kitchen. Cookies will be ready in a couple of minutes. What you would like to drink—iced tea, milk, soda?"

Dave turned on the charm. "Oh, Mrs. Wyler, I see now where your daughter gets her beauty from. And you must bake the world's best cookies, judging by the smell in here. I'd love some iced tea, if it's not too much bother."

Chantel chimed in: "Iced tea will be fine. Thanks, Mom."

Settled around the kitchen table, they snacked and chatted about the day's events. Mrs. Wyler asked them about *Sound of Music*, and what they thought of this old classic.

Dave commented first: "Well, I think it's sappy, and unbelievably innocent, but—you know, I still like it. I feel something in the music that makes me smile."

Chantel's response was, "The coaches are great,

and everyone in the cast has been terrific. Had no idea that acting could be so much fun!"

After taking another bite of her cookie, she continued: "Mom, *Sound of Music* is pure joy. Every song is delightful, but my absolute favorite is "Climb Ev'ry Mountain." What a beautiful and profound piece."

Mrs. Wyler murmured to her daughter, "Both happy and profound, that's exactly how I felt about that piece when I sang it in the play."

"Mom! You were in *Sound of Music*?"

"Yes—back in college. I was the Mother Superior."

"What? And you never told me—even after you knew we were doing the play?

"Sweetie, I wanted to be sure you had your own experience and discovery: didn't want you feeling that you had to audition to please me, or to copy what I did. What it means to you, *now,* is far more important than what I felt back then."

Dave cut in: "I think that's fantastic, Mrs. Wyler. Mother Superior, huh?"

"Yes, Dave. Delving into her character was an amazing experience—I loved that role!"

"Mrs. Wyler, I'd love to hear you sing *Climb Ev'ry Mountain*. Would you be willing to do that?"

"Maybe someday" she smiled, "but not till after your performance."

"Fair enough. I'll be looking forward to that."

Surprised by how quickly the afternoon had passed, Dave then made his polite goodbyes. Chantel walked him out to the car. "Thanks for the ride. See you at rehearsal."

Dave appeared uncharacteristically reflective. After a moment's hesitation he blurted out, "I'd really like to get to know you better. You're different from the other girls. And your Mom is something special! Can I drive you home tomorrow too?"

"Sure—the walk is OK, but it's nice to get a ride once in a while."

After that, whenever there was a rehearsal, Dave drove Chantel home afterward. Thus grew an unlikely, totally platonic friendship. He would tell her about his several girlfriends, enthusing about each one of them, then coming to Chantel for advice or suggestions when things didn't work out. Often he'd brag about his past accomplishments, or his plans for the future: "I've got an unbeatable plan. I can't lose!"

Under Dave's brash ego and obnoxious bravado was a frightened and insecure young man continually having to prove himself. Over many afternoons at their kitchen table, Dave had come to realize that both Chantel and her mother were sincere, trustworthy, and able to keep a confidence. He gradually let his guard down with them, revealing the real person underneath his cocksure persona.

Chantel, in turn, was overcoming her shyness—some of Dave's extroversion was rubbing off on her. At school she began greeting the other students with a warm smile, and after a while, even managed to participate in casual conversations without feeling awkward.

Opening night finally arrived. The play went wonderfully, and the audience gave them a standing ovation. Afterwards, the jubilant students exchanged hugs and high-fives backstage. Noisily packing into their cars, many of them headed off to the cast party to continue celebrating.

Dave had planned to join them. He started his car, turned on his favorite music, and drove off, his thoughts reliving the great performance that night. A few minutes later, he found himself in front of Chantel's house. That's not where he'd intended to go!

Instead of leaving, though, he spent a few minutes asking himself how and why he had ended up here instead of at the party. Suddenly the party seemed inconsequential. What awaited him in this modest, unassuming home was far more important, he realized.

He sprinted to the door and rang the bell. When a startled Sara answered, he blurted out, "You promised that you'd sing "Climb Ev'ry Mountain" for me sometime, Mrs. Wyler. Could you do it now, please?"

"Who is it, honey? Her husband called.

"It's Chantel's friend Dave—the one who played Captain von Trapp tonight."

She ushered him inside and gestured for him to sit on the couch. "Now, what's this all about?" she asked. "Shouldn't you be celebrating with the others?"

"That's where I thought I was going, but somehow I ended up here instead. You may have a hard time believing this, but while I was sitting in the car, it hit me that even though the cast did a great job, nobody really *gets* it except as a fun thing to do. They'll be partying and congratulating themselves on how terrific they were.

"*Sound of Music* is much more than just another

musical—it's an inspiration. I needed to be with someone who understands that and won't laugh at me for feeling this way."

"Of course we won't laugh at you, Dave. But what does that have to do with my singing?"

Having heard this exchange, Chantel quietly entered the living room and sat down on the piano bench.

"It's hard to explain, but all my life I've wanted to be a Hollywood star. You know—fame, lots of money, popularity. Now I just don't know. Talking with you and Chantel here in your house these last several weeks has been making me think. I'm changing into a different person. I find myself caring about other people instead of only me—this is a totally new thing."

He paused, looking down at his hands: "I know every word of every song in the play, but there's something missing. I think you know what it is, and if I could hear you sing, maybe I'd learn too. Please?"

Sara nodded, then smiled at her daughter, who was looking on with a mixture of bewilderment and anticipation. "Chantel, would you hit an 'E' for me? Thanks."

She took a moment to center herself, and then began singing. She had a glorious voice: as the rich tones of "Climb Ev'ry Mountain" filled the room, Dave and Chantel listened in rapt attention.

When the last notes rang out, nobody moved—no one wanted to break the silence. Finally, Chantel said, "Thank you, Mom. That was incredible!"

Nearly speechless, all Dave could manage was a

whispered, "Wow!"

After a long pause, Dave haltingly explained what he'd felt. "It was as though there was someone in the room, protecting and encouraging me to keep growing, to be the best person I know how to be.

"When I was a little kid my Mom told me I could do anything if I worked hard and set my mind to it. This felt a little bit like that, but more sweet and loving.

His voice dropped to a whisper. "It seemed…it seemed almost like a…like an angel."

Sara responded, "That's exactly what it was, Dave—your Guardian Angel was teaching you about the next steps in your life, and about your symbolic mountains to climb."

Startled out of his reverie, he said, "Huh? How do you know that? O God, are you one of those psychics who sees stuff in people and then snoops into their private lives?"

She smiled warmly. "No, Dave, I don't 'see stuff in people,' as you call it, and I certainly wouldn't pry into someone's personal affairs. Once in a while though, I get impressions—*just like you did* a few minutes ago. Tonight everything clicked: we felt the same thing. To me it was a 'Being of Light,' a warm, caring presence that was instructing me to be my best self always and to take joy in climbing the mountain of life."

She continued, "So you see, Dave, there is power in music. When sung with feeling, this piece can and does communicate inspiration and aspiration."

The three of them sat quietly for a few minutes, again reflecting on what this experience meant to each of them.

Dave rose, breaking the silence. "Mrs. Wyler, I just want you to know I'll remember this night the rest of my life, and when things get rough, its memory will carry me through. Good night, and thank you again."

She took his hand, holding it with both her own and gazing deeply into his eyes. "Good night, Dave. God be with you."

That simple but profound experience changed Dave permanently. Dropping his egocentric dream of instant fame and stardom, he began to encourage and help shy, withdrawn students at school. His goals changed drastically: he decided to go to college, taking theater arts and psychology courses in order to become a drama teacher, coach, and counselor for at-risk high school students.

Chapter 7
Becoming William

Billy got on the bus for the six-hour ride to the university. He still couldn't believe this was really happening. So many incredible changes, so fast!

As the bus rolled through the countryside, lulling many passengers to sleep, Billy found himself once again contemplating the significant conversations and events of the past year. He shook his head in amazement at the turns his life was taking.

❦ ❦ ❦

It had started with Mr. Altmer asking Billy about his plans after high school. Billy responded, "I guess I'll get a job somewhere. That's what people do, isn't it?"

"Have you considered going to college?"

"Me? Never—that's only for smart, rich people."

"You're plenty smart, Billy. When I was talking to Mr. Phelps yesterday, we both agreed you'd do well in Advanced Placement courses. Give them a try next semester. With some of those under your belt, you should have no problem getting into college."

"But college is expensive—I don't have family to help pay for anything."

"There's other ways—scholarships, loans, part-time work, even joining the armed services. Think about it, son."

"I will, sir."

Once again, he'd wondered about Mr. Altmer. He certainly didn't act like just a maintenance guy; even the Principal respected him and asked his advice. Quiet and patient as he was, it still seemed that he was used to being in command and being obeyed. Strange!

As summer ended, Billy took Mr. Altmer's advice and signed up for AP courses. To his surprise, he enjoyed the stimulating challenges they offered, and did well in classes. His favorite area was biology and related sciences: the mystery of life fascinated and intrigued him. With the encouragement of his teachers, he set a new goal of fulfilling the "impossible dream" of attending a university.

Throughout his senior year, he continued working with Mr. Altmer, who by this time had become a mentor and father figure to him. When Billy had problems or needed advice, he came to him for help. As he began developing hopes and ideals for his life, he shared these with Mr. Altmer alone.

When it came time to apply for scholarships, he

asked both Altmer and Phelps if they would write recommendations for him. They warmly agreed. Later the principal called him into the office to give him his letters. Billy skimmed them, then gasped on seeing Altmer's signature: Robert Altmer, COL, (USA Retired).

When the principal asked what was wrong, Billy stammered: "I just saw Mr. Altmer's signature. Did you know he was a Colonel?"

"Yes—he was my commanding officer."

"What!?"

Phelps smiled at him and said, "Billy, it's time for you to know something about Robert's background. Let me call him now so he can tell you himself."

A few minutes later, Altmer entered the office. Looking first at Mr. Phelps, then making direct eye contact with Billy, he said "Young man, what you're going to hear in this office must be kept in strict confidence. Tell no one. Will you give me your word of honor on that?"

"Of course I will!"

After they exchanged a firm handshake to confirm this, Phelps gestured them to seats around the desk.

Altmer began, "Well, Billy, I was in the Army for twenty years. My superiors apparently thought I was doing a good job, because they kept promoting me. When I first joined, it was satisfying. The Army taught me a lot, especially self-discipline, and I'm grateful for that.

As the years went on, though, it became harder and harder to reconcile this career with my vision of what life should really be about. In the service, my duties consisted mainly of teaching the arts of war; training people to blow up bridges, destroy cities, and kill each other in a hundred creative ways.

He nodded to the principal. "Mr. Phelps here was my assistant for two years. During that time we became close friends, despite our differences in rank. He saw what a struggle it was for me to continue this effort. After he returned to civilian life we kept in touch.

"When it came time for me to retire, I told him that I would no longer have anything to do with war, intrigue or power. The business world didn't seem right either, with its dog-eat-dog competitiveness. My dream was to work peacefully and harmoniously with the energies of life and renewal, not those of death and destruction.

"I'd already brought property in a remote area and was planning to build a little cabin miles away from anyone. But Phelps convinced me that I'd be more useful and needed here. He believed that in this humble position I could counsel and help students learn valuable skills and develop their God-given potential. He was right—it's been more rewarding than I ever thought possible."

Billy sat there, dumfounded. This man who was viewed by most of the students as just "the maintenance guy" (if they noticed him at all) had been a high-ranking officer! Billy had always appreciated Altmer's instruction and mentorship. But he now realized with new depth what a privilege this had been.

Mr. Phelps broke the silence. "Remember, Billy, nothing that we have said today must leave this office. We trust you to do that."

"I swear not to tell anyone."

Not long after, he received notice that he'd received a major scholarship. The first person he told was Mr. Altmer.

"Congratulations! I knew you could do it!" Altmer continued, "A new chapter in life, like this one, gives you a fresh start and almost unlimited choices. With your talent and hard work, you'll succeed at whatever you set your mind to doing."

Recalling that time in his own life, he reminisced, "When I left for college I decided to use my proper given name, 'Robert,' instead of being 'Bobby.' It was a simple thing, but made an immense difference—almost as though I had become a new person."

Altmer's remarks led Billy to look up the origins of his own name. On discovering that "William" means *resolute protector,* he felt a deep resonance with that name. He decided that, "Yes, that's what I'd like to be—a resolute protector."

⚜⚜⚜

The long bus ride finally ended. He walked to the designated meeting point on campus, where he was greeted by a member of the orientation team. She had the newcomers stand in a circle as she briefly explained the history of the university, then asked them each to introduce themselves and their reason for coming here. When his turn came, he straightened his shoulders and confidently stated: "My name is William—William Farragut. I'm here to start a new life."

CHANTEL'S SONG

Chapter 8
Nature's Inspiration

  Chantel took a brief break from studying to gaze out her dorm window at the distant hills. After a long cold winter, spring greens were beginning to emerge. Memories of delightful hikes with Kerrie swept over her. Best friends since high school, Chantel and Kerrie had shared many things, but most important of all, a love of nature. More than just pleasure, it was a deep appreciation of its blessings. "Better than any book," Kerrie was fond of saying, "and more interesting than most of our teachers. But if you want to learn, remember that nature doesn't use words. You've gotta open up with all of yourself. It's like hearing and seeing with your whole body."

  After a couple of years at the community college, Kerrie had gotten married and moved to Utah with her ranger husband and their new twins. She was also working on interpretive programs for the National parks. She'd called a few nights ago, bubbling with enthusiasm about developing a new wildlife parks program for city children. "This is so great! These kids have never even seen a running stream, or quail, or coyotes—just imagine the fun we'll all have!" By the time they hung up, Chantel knew it was time for her to get to the hills again. That would be her first priority when spring break came.

Now here it was, and on a crisp spring morning Chantel hiked through the hills, inhaling the crisp tang of pines and the richness of the soil where the snow had receded. Violets were popping up all around the trail, and on rounding a bend she encountered a tiny field of shooting stars.

She headed onward, then paused momentarily, not wanting to disturb the nearby finches in the brush. Glancing upward at a pair of hawks soaring on the thermals in the cloudless blue sky, she then opened her awareness to the varied bird serenades all around her. The "Wht,wht, wht" of quail she recognized easily. As for the rest, she tranquilly let them roll over her in harmonious sound.

Today she simply wanted to commune in nature's garden, not try to identify each species she saw or heard. Leave that to the scientists and the class assignments!

This was her time of just *being*, becoming re-filled with nature's harmony. She heaved a sigh of pure delight. It had been ever so long since she'd had the chance to take a walk in her beloved wilderness. For a while she forgot about school, the papers to finish, the exams to study for, the concert deadlines—this was heavenly. Every pore of her being drank up the peace and the tranquility of this special time.

Continuing her walk, she presently arrived at a

lookout point. Ahead, the hillside glowed chartreuse with blooming mustard, then flowed down to a vivid green expanse of willow-dotted meadow. Gentle breezes ruffled the leaves—were those sylphs dancing below? Surely if the bumblebees were there, some of her wee friends would be around too.

She chuckled to herself. How long had it been since she'd had thoughts like that? Now that Chantel was grown, she could no longer see the nature beings that had been her companions in childhood. Once in a great while she would hear their tinkling laughter or feel the slightest wisp of a hand stroking her face. Since her college classes had gotten so intense, though, even that contact was broken. "Maybe I'm the one who closed the door," she admitted ruefully.

As she proceeded, she felt as though her soul was being filled with peace, deeply appreciating such simple joys as the comforting warmth of rocks and lulling tempo of the winged symphony all around her.

Thoughts about school assignments intruded; "Oh yes, I've still got to compose a ballad for music theory, and the creative writing class needs a poem too. Well, I'm not going to worry about them now—not on this perfect day!"

After a couple of hours climbing a familiar route, Chantel heard the sound of water. Wanting to get closer to the source, she took a path that was new to her. Within minutes she arrived at a tiny cascading stream. She followed this and, in a few more turns of the path, discovered a hidden miniature waterfall. She stopped there, thrilled with its notes and crystalline sparkles. Alongside was a sun-warmed rock that was just the right

77

height for sitting. She settled with gratitude on the welcoming stone, totally relaxing in this place of hospitable beauty and deep peace.

Softly, a melody came into her consciousness—gentle and sweet, with a haunting harmony. She hummed it half a dozen times. There—now she'd remember for sure. She was already visualizing it on a score and hearing how it would sound as a flute piece—or maybe a recorder would bring a gentler tone?

Presently the words came too, and tears: this was a poignant love song. Her heart ached with the beauty of an intense sense of personal loss combined with a universal acceptance of a larger oneness. Wisps of memory stirred—could this be from a previous lifetime?

Hello, hello, hello, my love
I cannot say goodbye
But evermore will search above
Beyond the azure sky

The breezes, blowing, touch my face,
As gentle as your hand;
Their distant sighing notes of grace
I stretch to understand.

Rejoice, my love, you're free from pain
And finished now with strife
With peace and strength and freedom gained
May blessings fill your life.

As she softly sang the piece, she realized it would be perfect for both of her school assignments. With great joy, she flashed a smile of thanks to the nature presences who had given her this song. Even though she could no longer see them, her childhood contact with the nature beings left indelible memories. She knew she couldn't go back to that pure innocence, but clearly remembered the comfort and sheer delight they'd given her. Childhood had been lovely, but certainly adulthood had many compensatory joys, she reflected.

Chapter 9
THEY MEET AGAIN

Chantel had finished her first student counseling session: her next appointment wasn't till 11, so she decided to take a little break at her favorite coffee shop. As she entered, William looked up from his corner table, did a classic double-take, and awkwardly pointed a finger in her direction. "I know you!"

She was momentarily startled, but recovered quickly. She replied coolly but with a slight twinkle in her eye, "That's not a very original line."

He gestured for her to join him, insisting, "No, I really do know you—I'm sure of it! We've met before—but where?"

Chantel quickly assessed this young man with the rumpled dark hair and penetrating brown eyes. He obviously had strong convictions and was quite genuine. No smooth-talking persona here. What you saw was what you got!

"I'm William—William Farragut. C'mon, let's figure this out."

She paused, glanced at her watch—still some time before she had to head back to work—and decided it wouldn't hurt to talk for a few minutes with this intense, direct stranger. His eyes sparkled with lively determination. She got her coffee and sat down across the table from him. Smiling, she said, "Hi, William. My name is Chantel."

With that they proceeded to compare possibilities. They found they had both grown up here in Veronia, but had gone to different schools and led very different lives.

She was a singer and teacher, a churchgoer who had lived here all her life, except for her college years. Her kind, loving family had always been tremendously supportive and appreciative of her talents and efforts.

He'd grown up as a neglected child, staying in a series of foster homes after his mother abandoned him. He'd left town as soon as he could, continuing his education out of state. Today was his first day back here since high school.

Although they determined they couldn't have met earlier, Chantel too was struck by a sense of familiarity; an unlikely kinship with this thoughtful yet very deliberate man, so different from herself.

His experiences with life had been hard; without a caring family, he'd had to learn about life all on his own. He told Chantel that he'd been gone for several years studying at college, working several part-time jobs, mainly as a repairman or mechanic. Gradually he found that he could detect problems and discover solutions simply by running his hands over objects. Somehow it was as if his hands could actually "feel" the problem and work out the solution.

"I worked in an animal hospital one summer. I enjoyed that a lot, and the veterinarian told me that the animals always got better when I was taking care of them. He encouraged me to go to Veterinary School, and I finally did. Took my internship in Chicago: the partners asked me to join their practice afterward."

He paused to sip his coffee, then continued. "I was all set to do that. One day, though, it was like a voice told me, 'It's time to come home now—and time to begin your Real Work.' So here I am. I know that sounds weird," he said, turning his hands up and spreading them on the table, "but it's God's honest truth."

"No, it doesn't seem weird to me," Chantel replied thoughtfully. "I've heard that kind of voice too, and I've found it's very important to listen to it."

He looked warily at her. "You don't think I'm crazy, then? Folks at work thought I was nuts when I'd say stuff like that. After a while I learned to shut up—got tired of being bugged all the time."

"Some people would call it "intuition," or "listening to your inner promptings," she responded. "What do you do when you hear the voice?"

"Well, things always turn out better when I do what it says. So by now I pay attention."

She regarded him calmly. "Do you have any notion of what this "Real Work" of yours is intended to be?"

"Nope—all I know is that when it comes, I'll know it."

Chantel smiled. "Yes, you will indeed." She paused, with a bewildered expression on her face. "That's strange—I've never had such a sureness about anyone else's future, let alone someone I just met."

She finished her coffee and rose. "It's time for me to get back to work now, William. Good luck with your project."

"Hey, hey, slow down! You're the first person who listens to me without thinking that I belong in the loony bin—you can't just up and leave. I've got to see you again…please?"

"William, this has been a nice break. I've enjoyed talking with you, but I've got an 11 o'clock appointment. Bye!"

"But how will I ever find you?"

"Use your intuition," she whispered, lightly touching his hand on her way out.

He sat there, momentarily stunned. Someone at last had listened to him, really listened, and then, in a blink, she was gone. Shaking his head to clear it—maybe he'd imagined the whole thing—William got up to leave.

"Excuse me, but do you know that young lady, the one that was having coffee with me?" he asked the bored-looking teenager behind the counter.

"Huh-uh."

"She ever been here before?" he persisted.

"Dunno. I only been workin' here a coupla weeks," the boy mumbled.

William started out the door, only to be stopped by a "Hey, where d'ya think you're goin'! You haven't paid your bill yet!"

"Oh—sorry! How much do I owe you?"

"Hang on a minute. I'll add it up…stupid machine needs more paper." After a few more minutes, "OK, here ya go."

By the time William paid and got outside, Chantel was nowhere in sight.

"Use your intuition," she'd said. OK then, by God, he'd do just that.

Ignoring the passersby on the sidewalk and the steady stream of roadside traffic, William stood quietly outside the coffee shop, closed his eyes and tried to empty his mind of all the confusion and busyness that surrounded him. This was surprisingly easy for him—modified from a technique he'd discovered in childhood. Ever since he was a little kid he'd been able to stop and "find a still place inside," as he'd always called it. The worse that things had been in his outer world, the more often he had come to "the still place."

He remembered doing that with Hooshee by his side, once again feeling the steady faithfulness of his long-departed dog. Into his waiting stillness came an image—a white wooden building, surrounded by a crisp well-manicured lawn. In a relaxed way, he mentally scanned the area, noticing two symmetrical maple trees arching over a graceful, curved path to the building. Then in his mind's ear, he heard bells. Of course! Snapping out of his reverie, he almost laughed at the clarity of the final image—a spire and a white bird. Pretty darn obvious that it had to be a church. The town wasn't that big; how long could it possibly take to find that particular building?

He'd been in church only once in his life. When he was about seven years old, a neighbor, saying she was concerned about his eternal welfare, dragged him to a cold gray building where a man in fancy robes scolded them all, calling them evil sinners and yelling about fire and brimstone and eternal punishment for evildoers. The only thing that impressed him at the time was how long the man could go on shouting nonstop. He'd been thoroughly bored, and truth to tell, a tiny bit frightened. After an interminable time fidgeting on the seat, he'd finally been free to go outside and breathe fresh clean air again. What a confining, constricting, *grim* place that had been!

Meanwhile, back to the present day and the challenge of finding Chantel. Once he'd located the church, he figured he'd have to sit through another long shouting ordeal, but then perhaps could get a chance to talk to her afterwards.

It took three weeks, but having finally found the building that matched his image, William sat in the back of a simple unpretentious church on Sunday morning. He crossed his arms, waiting none too patiently for the service to start. The sooner it began, the quicker he'd be able to find Chantel. He looked around—the place looked light and airy. Gradually people arrived, smiled warmly at him, and then took their seats, apparently looking forward to the service with eagerness. Once again he contrasted that with his childhood experience— these people certainly didn't look as though they'd been dragged here to be punished. He filed that thought away under "Examine later."

He also remembered that she'd said she loved to sing. "OK then, Chantel," he promised himself, "I'm gonna hear you sing, somewhere, somehow—even if I have to look all over the state."

Just then the choir entered, singing joyfully. His breath caught as he saw Chantel in the group, her blonde hair shining like a halo. He'd never heard such happy music, nor seen such radiant faces.

"Yes," his inner voice rang out, "Yes, yes, yes!"

CHANTEL'S SONG

Chapter 10
Deeper Sharing

William and Chantel arrived at the lakeside restaurant for an early dinner. It was a sunny spring afternoon, glowing with a promise of summer.

The receptionist led them to a table with a broad view of both the lake and the park-like landscape. After they were seated, William pointed to a hummingbird sipping nectar from a trumpet vine blossom very near them.

Chantel said, "How lovely—that means there's an angel nearby." William smiled indulgently at what he perceived as poetic imagery. She protested, "You look like you're just humoring me. But it's true!"

"No, I—well, how about telling me why you think there's an angel?"

She paused, took a deep breath, and then hesitantly explained that when she was a little girl she could see and hear some things that other children couldn't. There were tiny shimmering beings darting through the grass, caressing the flowers, laughing in the wind. Larger ones busied themselves around or within trees and boulders.

Chantel continued, "When I asked Mom what they were, she told me that they were nature's invisible helpers, and had all sorts of different names. She said that since most people couldn't see them, they often didn't believe these were real…Two of them, Shana and Griff, were my best friends. I haven't thought of them in years, but they were constant companions in our back yard when I was a little girl." Noticing William's bemused expression, she sighed. "Oh dear, you don't believe me, do you?"

William gazed at this animated, beautiful girl who could, with total conviction, say the most surprising things. He couldn't help but smile at her enthusiasm and love of life.

Chantel continued, her face suddenly lighting up, "But I remember, just as though it was yesterday, when Shana and Griff showed me one of the angels that are always around hummingbirds. There was a hummingbird nest in an oak tree. The most beautiful angel, shining and serene, was nearby. She sheltered and protected the adults as well as the eggs, and then the hatchlings.

"Shana and Griff explained that there are different angels that look out for each type of animal—the birds have their own helpers, the wild creatures in the forest have theirs, and there is a special type of angel whose responsibility is taking care of domestic animals who have gotten lost and need a new home."

A long-forgotten childhood memory tugged at William's mind. Suddenly it came back in full detail: A stormy night when he was nine, a bedraggled dog at the front door, and the brief vision of a brilliantly shining presence communicating love, warmth, and reassurance.

He burst out: "Oh my God—of course! That's what it was!"

"That's what *what* was? What are you talking about, William?"

Reluctantly at first, then with gradually increasing confidence, he told her about that night and the Presence that had brought his dog Hooshee to him. As a child he'd never told anyone about it: he knew his mother would be too tired to listen, and the other kids would think he was crazy. Gradually the memory of the experience faded. By adulthood he had forgotten that dramatic night, until this very moment.

Chantel smiled with understanding. "Just like Shana and Griff said—that must have been one of the angels that guides lost pets to their new home where they'll be loved."

Chantel's words lifted his spirits—he was immensely relieved that what he'd seen and heard as a boy was true, not a symptom of mental imbalance.

Just then dinner arrived. It was beautifully presented and delicious. Their appreciation of the meal diverted the conversation to pleasant but more mundane subjects. Afterwards, Chantel and William strolled along the shoreline, then settled down on a hand-carved wooden bench. They watched the sun set and then sat quietly listening to the sounds of nature as the earth prepared for evening.

Presently, William said, "I've been thinking about what you said. I'm feeling unusually calm and peaceful here. Do you suppose there's something like a lake nature being nearby?"

Her response was, "You can feel it too? That's wonderful, and *of course* there must be a water being watching over this lake. Shana and Griff used to tell me how beautiful and graceful these nature beings are, and about the peace and serenity that they project into the atmosphere—not just at the lake itself but in a wide range all around it."

William nodded slowly, absorbing her words as he continued to feel an ever-deepening peace. After a few moments, he began, almost unconsciously, humming a soft, sweet melody. Chantel's eyes widened in surprise. "William—that tune…how do you know it? Where did you hear it?"

"This? I've known it forever. When I was a kid and feeling lonely or sad, the song would come, and soon I'd be feeling better.

"Funny, it always seemed as though a beautiful lady or an angel was singing it to me—just to me. It made me feel as though I belonged to someone and had a safe place to be."

"Does the next line sound like this?" she asked, continuing the poignant melody.

Now it was William's turn to be astonished. "Wha… how could you possibly know that?"

She explained how it came to her while she was a student, taking a brief break in the mountains. After a moment, she added, "Even then I had a premonition that this wasn't just a song, but would mean something very significant in my life."

"And what about the words?" asked William.

She blushed and stammered, "Er, um, they…I can't…not now."

"So you won't tell me?"

"Not won't—*can't*. The words are locked within my heart: I haven't been given permission to release them yet."

William squeezed her hand reassuringly. "It's all right—perhaps someday."

She smiled at him. "Yes, William, I truly believe that someday you'll be the one to hear the words."

They remained on the bench until the twilight faded, then returned to the car, both deep in their own thoughts and memories.

Chapter 11
OUT OF THE PAST

The neatly groomed man strode into the vet's office with his dog, an aging golden retriever wearing a service dog vest. On the firm command of, "Courage, *down*," the dog settled calmly at his master's side.

William happened to be covering the front office for an hour while the receptionist was at lunch. He began to record intake information concerning the medical history of the retriever, as well as his current symptoms. Suddenly the dog's owner smiled broadly in recognition. "Billy! Billy Farragut! It's Joe!"

William looked up with a puzzled expression. "Excuse me? Nobody's called me Billy since I graduated from high school. It's William now. Do I know you?"

"Back in school—I made life miserable for you, and I'm sure you must have hated my guts."

After staring blankly at the man's face for a while, memories came flooding back. In a carefully neutral tone, he said, "Oh, yeah, Joe—I remember you all right. But you've changed so much it took a while to recognize you."

"Billy…William, I can't tell you how glad I am to have met up with you again. First of all, I need to apologize for my awful behavior in school." Sticking out his hand, he continued, "I was rotten to you when we were kids. The things I said and did were despicable, and I'm truly sorry. Can you—will you—forgive me?"

William was baffled. Through his work, he'd learned that a man's character could be dependably judged by how he treated his dog, and the dog's feelings about him. Yet here was this tormentor from high school who obviously loved his dog, caring for him with kindness and respect. And the dog clearly adored him.

After a pause, William nodded cautiously, then warily put out his own hand to shake the proffered one. Then he reiterated, "I still don't understand. What happened to change you so much? You're totally transformed!"

Joe replied: "The story's much too long to tell right now, and I'm not sure you'd believe it, my friend. But I'm not the same person you knew in high school." They made eye contact for a long moment, Joe finally nodding as though he'd seen something that helped him come to a decision. "If you really want to know, let's have lunch together some day."

"Yeah, I'd like to hear your story." Glancing at his calendar for verification, he said, "I can free up some time tomorrow afternoon."

"Works for me. 12:30? The old coffee shop at First and Ash?"

"That'll be fine. Now let's get back to your dog, Courage, and the reason you came here."

Courage wagged his tail throughout the exam, licking William's hand enthusiastically. After asking a few more questions, William commented, "Looks like we'll need some tests to find out exactly what's going on with the old boy." Rather than asking directly why Joe needed a service dog, he just said, "If you're OK being without him for a while, let's keep him here overnight. Should have some answers by tomorrow."

"I'll miss him, but sure, keep him overnight if that's what you need to find out what's wrong with him."

The next day, Joe came to pick up Courage, who turned out to have nothing worse than a touch of arthritis. After greeting his owner with slurps and enthusiastic tail-wagging, and having his service vest put on again, Courage accompanied the two men to the coffee shop. Once there, they requested a table way in back so they could have enough time to speak privately without interruptions. Courage settled in underneath the table, laying his head on Joe's feet.

After they had both ordered, William and Joe sat quietly for a few minutes. William finally broke the silence with, "What was it you were going to tell me?"

Joe took a deep breath, let it out with a whoosh, and began.

"Ever since I remember, I had to make myself feel better than the other kids. In grade school I'd be making fun of little runts, or of kids who talked funny, or had big ears, or whatever. Teasing them and feeling their fear and misery gave me a sense of power. After a while I started

Chantel's Song

shaking down the younger ones so they'd give me their lunch money. I didn't do it for the money—but seeing their little faces, knowing they were too scared to tell anybody, was a real rush.

"My buddies were just as much into bullying as I was. With every threat and success, we'd slap each other on the back and congratulate ourselves on how tough we were. "Man, did you see that guy squirm? We really got him, didn't we?" Of course, we'd compete to see who could go the farthest before getting caught. Bigger, tougher, meaner, smarter—that was our motto.

"We soon found out it only took a few threats to keep kids in line. After that we changed methods, specializing in getting them to do the dirty work for us. That was great! Even though we'd make them break into abandoned houses for us, or maybe do a little shoplifting, we could still truthfully tell the police, 'Oh no, sir. I've never set foot in the place.' We thought we were so clever!"

William stared across the table at Joe. A vague childhood memory suddenly became crystal clear. "That was you, wasn't it, Joe, at the old Caslan house? You're the one who gave Ralph the idea of getting me to go in the door that had a loose board. You told him I was the only one small enough to squeeze through. Once he decided it was his own idea and not yours, he tried to get me to open the front door for the rest of you.

As Joe nodded, William continued. "You all made fun of me then—made me feel like a coward if I didn't do what you wanted, so I did manage to get in the house. I played a few notes on the dusty old piano; then before I could open the door for you guys, I heard a loud, 'Billy, stop. Don't do this.' Then my dog showed up, howling his head off, so I grabbed him and took him home just as that awful storm began."

Joe's eyes had gotten wide with William's story. "That's the sort of thing I did all the time. I remember telling the guy in middle school—his name was Ralph, you say?—that "the runt" should go inside first and then open the door for everyone else. What happened next though, was scary. Here's the way I remember it. There was eerie music coming from inside the house, and a booming voice saying something that I couldn't understand. I could have sworn the house itself was talking. Finally, I heard footsteps and an awful wailing, panting, and scuffling. There was a light too. The place really had to be haunted! We got out of there as fast as we could."

"Wait a second—you said you saw a light? Where? What did it look like?"

"It was by the loose board just outside the house—it was gold-colored, like a bonfire, but there was no fire, no flames."

"That's the same light I saw!" William confirmed.

They stared at each other for a long moment in silence, each reliving what they'd seen so long ago. Then Joe continued; "I didn't believe that then; figured it had to be some kind of weird burglar alarm at the old place.

The waitress brought their lunch, temporarily stopping the conversation. "Anything else I can getcha?"

They both shook their heads, William murmuring, "No, we're fine, thanks." They ate quietly for a while before Joe resumed.

"By the time you knew me in high school, William, I was a hardened delinquent—but most of the teachers didn't realize it yet. Remember the day we got called to the principal's office?"

William responded, "Do I ever! Never wanted to go through that again—it was like Mr. Phelps could see right through us to the truth. I was scared that he'd be able to see everything I'd ever done. You know, though, I'm glad he sent us to Mr. Altmer. That was one of the best things that happened to me in school."

Joe smiled: "Altmer tried really hard to teach me practical skills. I thought he was stupid and naive. He was just the maintenance guy, after all! Figured I could slack off and he wouldn't notice. Of course I was dead wrong. Still, the harder he tried to work with me, the more stubborn I got."

"Well, Joe, my experience with Mr. Altmer was just the opposite. He was the first person in my life who cared what I thought, who ever really listened to me. I never knew my dad, but always imagined a father would do that, and would teach by example, and would trust his son to do the right thing.

"He gave my life direction—let me know I could make goals and achieve them. He believed in me. It was because of him that I was able to go to college."

Joe responded, "I realize now how patient Mr. Altmer was, and what a good role model he was, but at the time I didn't want anything to do with him. You may remember I bugged out after a week or so. Never went back to that school again. I hung out on the streets here for a while, then moved over to Grayville and was doing drugs with new pals. I was only 15, but since school was where they kept trying to tell you what to do, I figured I didn't need any more of it. Neither the truant officer nor the judge saw things that way, though.

"Although many people warned me about the path I was taking, I ignored their advice—what did they know? I got so much energy from making people squirm and beg: what a rush! Short story long, I ended up in the alternative school system for a while. There were some remarkable teachers there, trying to get it through my thick head that I was heading the wrong way. But did I listen? No way!

"As soon as I turned 16, I was outta there. Now I could finally do what I wanted to do—come up with ever more brilliant ways of outsmarting the law and supporting my drug habit. When I got caught, I'd do my time in juvenile hall. I was pretty cocky, and each time learned how to work the system even more.

He paused for a sip of water. "So many people tried to help—teachers, counselors, probation officers, judges—but I wasn't about to listen to them. No one was going to boss me around, tell me what to do.

"William, these were *good* people, doing their very best. They genuinely tried to get through to me, but I never listened. Instead, I'd be thinking, 'You boring, stupid idiots. I'm much smarter than you'll ever be.' Actually, the language was much more vulgar, but you get the picture."

William interrupted: "Yeah, Joe, whatever happened to your language? I haven't heard you use a single swear word since you started talking today. You sure don't sound like the old Joe I knew."

"Well, let's just say that since I've learned the

power of words, and thoughts, I'm much more careful about how I use them.

"After I got too old for juvie, I'd tell the judge whatever he wanted to hear—faking remorse, apologizing, the whole nine yards. That usually got me a reduced sentence; a month in jail, probation, that sort of thing. By now I was getting really good at stealing cars; pulled off some clever armed robberies, got off scot-free.

"As time went on I got even more skilled and better organized. I thought nothing could stop me. I was tough as nails: by now I had my own guys to do the dirty work. Usually threats kept them in line, but I'd occasionally make an example of someone. They'd show up in an alley with stab wounds, or sometimes just mysteriously disappear. Power was the most important thing to me. That gave me a high that was even better than drugs.

"Once in a while the judges would try to talk sense into me, but I was cocky. I used their advice all right—to figure out new ways to play their 'law' game and win every time. Parole officers and counselors couldn't reach me either: I knew what I wanted in life, and it certainly didn't involve what those idiots said—not when I was so much smarter than them.

"Finally people quit trying to rehab me: I ended up doing hard time in the state penitentiary. When I couldn't be the top boss anymore, I got in stupid fights with the other inmates: ended up in solitary. After two weeks with no one to talk to, I hit bottom. I was yelling, cursing everybody I could think of: the cops, the guys who ratted on me, the lawyers, probation officers, judges, chaplains, the system, God—if there was one. Finally, when I was too worn out and hoarse to yell anymore, I collapsed into a corner of the cell."

He choked up momentarily. Gradually regaining control, he said, "What I'm about to tell you sounds crazy, but please hear me out…It's impossible to put this experience into words. The whole thing seems melodramatic and unbelievable, but I swear what happened is absolutely true.

"Despair and hopelessness saturated every thought, every feeling, every molecule. The blackest black you could imagine came over me—sucking out all of what I considered to be *me*. I was falling into a bottomless pit with no hope of ever getting out, of ever being able to breathe, think, or even live. It was as though I was no longer *being*. I would have given anything to be a slug, a weed, a rock, anything, simply to know that I still existed in some form. This deep *nothingness* may have lasted only a moment, but it felt like an eternity.

"And then…there was a voice, deep and powerful. It reverberated through all of space, yet was addressing me alone. 'Joe. You must choose **now**. Where is your allegiance—Good or Evil?

'If you deliberately embrace evil, you'll have all the power, you want. You'll be absolute boss of this whole prison; when you get out, you'll be rich, powerful, influential, successful—everything this world offers can be yours.

'But what you've felt now is just a sample of the terror, the absence, the no-thing-ness that awaits you at the end. When one turns away from God, there is nothing.'

"Although I couldn't comprehend what was happening, the voice gave me an anchor in the darkness. If I could hear this *something* or *someone* talking to me, it meant that there was an "I" to be aware of it. At the same time there came a waft of air. I gasped, filling my lungs with the precious stuff. Thank God—I had lungs, so I had a physical body again.

"That very realization shocked me into gratitude, and with that came a distant glimmer of light. The voice continued: 'If you choose the Good, it won't be easy at first. You will have to make amends for all the harm you've caused to people. You will have to endure the same pain you put them through, but the strength of your soul will light the way. There will be testings—there are always challenges in this earthly life—but you will be given the help and the tools you need to deal with them.'

"The Light was closer now and increasing in brightness. 'The decision is yours alone, Joe. Which will it be—Good or evil?'

"Within the Light, I became aware of a pair of eyes piercing through to my essence, and a glowing sword. This Being (I could only assume He was an Angel) offered the sword for me to use in making the choice.

"Then I saw two roads to the future opening up before me. One showed what looked like the glittering lights of Las Vegas, glamorous showgirls, immense wealth, more pleasure and power than I could imagine. But beyond that was only an inky black void. The other was a rocky, barren path leading upward to a mountaintop. As I looked more closely at this option, the landscape changed. It offered refreshing waters, expansive prairies, sheltering forests, breathtaking beauty. At the top was a Light glorious beyond description. Once at the summit, I knew there would be a 360-degree view not only of the mountain itself, but also of the complete terrain. I could see those who were on the path and had a clear vision of the entire journey. Beyond that was an incredible panorama of yet more wondrous, incredibly beautiful mountains glowing with radiance. It was as if they were calling, drawing me to them.

"As I made the choice, looked into those marvelous eyes, and reached out to grasp the sword hilt, the Voice resounded: 'Go forth in valor!' Then the Light blazed up yet again, filling the universe...That's the last thing I remember.

"They found me later, comatose, in the cell. Regulations said any prisoner found unconscious must have a medical exam, so they took me to the infirmary. There was nothing wrong with me, but they couldn't let it go, so ended up taking me for a neurological consult. The specialists finally diagnosed me with a seizure disorder of some sort.

"O gosh, William, look at the time. You've got to get back to work. Gimme thirty seconds to wind up. Short version: I changed 180 degrees, was released early for good behavior. Left the state to get a new start; worked to save money, then went to college there—even got a scholarship. After graduating, I continued training. Now I'm a counselor for troubled teens. These are the toughest cases. It's their one last chance—I call them the OLC kids."

"Joe—that's amazing! And I do believe you. Your diagnosis also explains why a young, apparently healthy guy like you needs a service dog.", responded William.

105

"Oh yeah! I've never had a major experience like that again, but once in a great while I get brief mild episodes. Courage lets me know when there's an impending small seizure. That gives me time to lie down. But Courage is much more than a service dog: he's an amazing, loyal companion."

Courage came out from under the table and licked Joe's hand. Joe patted him lovingly and said, "Hey Courage, you're a special friend, aren't you, buddy? Time to go!"

The men shook hands, promising to get together another time to continue their sharing.

Back at work, William reflected on the day's events. In yesterday's brief conversation, there had been closure to the unresolved relationships from years ago. But today, William was far beyond forgiveness—he felt honored to be entrusted with Joe's story, and truly rejoiced in his transformation.

Chapter 12
MEETING THE FAMILY

    William and Chantel drove out to the countryside where she'd grown up, and where her folks still lived. The poplar trees along the road were turning golden, hinting at autumn's early arrival.

    "It'll be the next left turn, William—just beyond that big pine tree up ahead."

    "OK—got it," he acknowledged, flicking the turn indicator on.

    As they turned onto the narrow side road, Chantel indicated the modest frame house, white with dark green trim, at the very end. They pulled up the driveway and parked. William got out first, coming around to open the door for Chantel. Taking a deep breath of crisp, cold air, he paused a moment before saying, "Wow—what a special place you grew up in! Funny, it doesn't look very different from the other places around, but it sure feels different—friendly and welcoming. No wonder you loved it so much as a kid."

Off to the side was a crabapple tree, its foliage a brilliant orange-bronze. He gestured to it. "Even this tree is part of the welcome!"

Chantel squeezed William's hand as they stepped onto the front porch. She bubbled enthusiastically: "Oh William, my parents will be thrilled to meet you. I've been telling them about you for quite a while now—Mom can hardly wait, and Dad is really looking forward to this evening too."

Just as she reached up to ring the bell, the door opened and Mr. Wyler greeted them: "Come in, come in—get warm!" Chantel made quick introductions on the porch. The men shook hands with a brief, "How do you do—it's a pleasure to meet you." Seeing her mother waiting just inside, Chantel slipped through the doorway to hug her.

Once they were in the living room, Mrs. Wyler also shook hands with William, holding it in both her own for a moment while looking directly into his eyes. "Welcome, William; we're so happy that you've come."

Meanwhile, Chantel's Dad wrapped her in a huge bear hug. In mock protest, she exclaimed, "Oof, Dad—I love you too, but let me catch my breath!"

William and Chantel dropped off their coats and settled down in the living room with her parents. After exchanging a few pleasantries Mrs. Wyler excused herself to check on dinner preparations. Chantel jumped up to help her in the kitchen.

For a while, Tom and William continued to chat about the weather and the drive over, but soon the conversation moved to Tom's fond reminiscences of his daughter's childhood. "She was just the cutest thing, always making up songs that she said she heard out in the trees. She was so funny and so sweet. I remember how she'd go out and play in the back yard, then come in all excited and tell us about her imaginary playmates, just as though they were real. She even gave them names!"

Mrs. Wyler entered the room just then, softly correcting her husband: "Honey, she wasn't imagining things—she really did see and hear them."

"Whatever you say, sweetheart—but wasn't she the prettiest little girl you'd ever seen? And look at her now—absolutely gorgeous!"

Then, turning back to William, he continued, "I hope you know what a special treasure Carol Ellen—I mean Chantel—is. Funny thing: one day when she was eight or so, Carol Ellen told us, out of the blue, 'My real name is Chantel.' Kids come up with the darndest things, don't they? Anyhow, she was determined that she was going to be Chantel from then on. That's a pretty name, but in my heart she'll always be my special baby Carol Ellen."

A timer went off in the kitchen. Mrs. Wyler said, "That means dinner's ready. Shall we?"

They stood up and moved to the dining room where Mrs. Wyler gestured them to their seats. Mr. Wyler said they'd like to offer a simple grace for the meal. He began, then paused so his wife could finish it.

This gesture of shared prayer charmed William, touching him deeply. He'd never heard grace before. Recalling his own childhood, he remembered that he and his mother had almost never sat together at the table for meals. Most often, food was an eat-and-run affair that involved grabbing something from the fridge and heading out the door. He remembered making peanut butter sandwiches and once in a while eating them at the kitchen table. If his mother meandered in, he'd ask her if she wanted some. Her usual response was, "Ugh, no. Is there any milk in the fridge?" More often than not, this would be followed by, "This tastes awful, and no wonder. Don't you ever check the date on the carton?"

Nothing in his childhood had prepared him for the friendly, peaceful, contented feeling at this table. The food was homemade and flavorful. William savored every bite. Conversation was comfortable and natural, covering a variety of topics.

Chantel's parents were intrigued and charmed by this sincere young man who obviously was in love with their daughter. He was respectful but not intimidated by them; he seemed to be genuinely interested in their thoughts and ideas. And how happy Chantel was—simply glowing with joy!

"This is delicious, Mrs. Wyler," William noted, taking another serving of still-steaming lasagna. "Italian food is one of my favorites."

"Thank you, William—the sauce was made from tomatoes, garlic and herbs that we grew in our garden last summer. Home-grown vegetables always seem to taste better than those you buy at the store."

Chantel chimed in. "Mom's been gardening for years; her garden is the happiest one on the block."

"The *happiest* garden?"

She nodded. "Exactly—Mom's garden makes you happy to be in it, and the plants grow better than they do in the other yards around. In spring and summer, if you listen really close, you can hear the veggies growing—it's a really soft humming. And no, it's not bees or bugs, it's the plants themselves doing it."

Tom chimed in "There she goes again—such a creative imagination! Plants humming—only our Carol would come up with that."

Smiling at her husband, Sara corrected him, "*Chantel* always tells the truth. If she says she hears something, she hears it."

"Sure, but come on now—humming?"

William, not knowing whether to be amused or concerned, glanced over at Chantel. She was smiling indulgently at her parents, her relaxed body language indicating that this was an old topic and that their differences of opinion were all in good humor.

After the meal, they settled down in the living room. Tom then turned to William, shifting from the friendly banter of the family to a mode of analytic questioning. "Carol—*Chantel*—tells us you have a unique way of treating animals at your clinic. What's so different about it?"

"It's not so unusual—it's just very satisfying to work with animals as patients."

"From what Chantel has said, there's something *mighty* different. She says you get miraculous results—much better than the other animal hospitals around here. There has to be a reason for that, young man."

William hesitated, having an inborn sense of

caution about revealing details of his personal beliefs. But after hearing the family's open discussion and acceptance of Chantel's perceptions, he decided to take the risk.

Taking a big breath, he began, "Well, sir, I'm not sure this will make sense to you, but most of the veterinarians I know, including the instructors who taught me, are really good at what I call 'mechanics.' They analyze animals the way a mechanic examines cars, using their mental check list to diagnose what's wrong, and then get in there to do repairs. They fix the animal's bodies as best they can, but often they really can't tell what's wrong. After all, our patients can't talk!"

Tom nodded, adding in a deliberately neutral tone, "Go on."

"I've found a way to communicate with the animals nonverbally. It sounds strange, I know, but they communicate with pictures, and as I gently run my hands along the back of a dog or cat, it will send images to my mind. It works the other way too—as long as I'm in physical contact, I can 'speak' in pictures and the animal will understand."

"Surely you don't mean you really believe you can communicate with them—they're just animals, after all," Tom responded. "You can't possibly be serious!"

"Sir, I'm absolutely serious, but I certainly can't blame you for not believing me. Let's just let this sit on the shelf awhile, OK?"

Mr. Wyler remained polite, but his tone was noticeably colder. "No, let's not. I'd like to check out this claim of yours right now. Are you up for it?"

"It sounds as though you're asking me to do a

parlor show, Mr. Wyler. Sorry, but I don't do those."

"And still you expect us to believe you?"

"It's the truth, sir."

"Then prove it!"

The women were shocked by the out-of-character hostility in Mr. Wyler's voice. Chantel spoke first, trying to placate him. "Dad, whatever you may think of his methods, William is a most amazing veterinarian—you should see the animals, and talk to their delighted owners, at his office."

Mrs. Wyler then tactfully redirected the conversation, suggesting they move to the living room to relax by the warmth of the stone fireplace. The moment they had settled down there, a huge Russian Blue cat entered, circling the room once, as if to claim it as hers, then made a beeline for William's lap.

As she relaxed there, William stroked her and murmured almost to himself, "Hello Katya. How are you this evening?"

Her response was a full-length stretch, followed by a rumbling purr.

Tom and Sarah stared in surprise. Their cat had always been spooked by strangers, running away to hide if anyone else came into the house. It was unheard of for Katya to actively seek out someone's lap and stay there so peacefully.

"Well, young man, I grant you have a gift with animals—she's never done anything like this before," Mr. Wyler commented in a much milder tone. "But how did you guess her name? Did Car—Chantel—tell you?"

"No sir, Katya told me herself. She also let me know that she really loves lying by the fireplace, whether or not there's a fire going. She tells me that you usually have a plaid blanket there for her to cozy up in."

"Hmm, I still can't believe that the cat told you, but, on the remote chance that it's true, how does she describe this blanket?"

William responded clearly and deliberately, "She's showing me lots of blue and green squares, each about the size of one of her paws, with thinner lines of gray between them. My guess is that the "gray" is really red, because cats are colorblind to red; they would see that as gray. She also is communicating that it's really soft and comfy because it gets folded up several times—oh, and it has a fringe that tickles her once in a while."

Sara moved to a nearby closet, returning with a fuzzy blue and green plaid throw intersected with fine lines of red. She shook it out to reveal the fringe, remarking quietly, "Is this what Katya showed you?"

She then folded it into a thick pad and placed it near the hearth. The cat, as if on cue, strolled over and curled up on her throw. Within a few minutes she was dozing serenely.

Smiling gently at the confusion evident on her Dad's face, Chantel touched his hand and told him, "Katya's confirming this, Dad. William truly does communicate with animals."

Tom's former hostility was replaced by mystification as he looked at Chantel. "Is this kind of like your imaginary friends then, baby? You tried to tell me they were real, but of course they couldn't be—could they?"

"Dad, there are so many things we can't explain with our five senses, but they're just as real as anything we see or hear right in this room. For example, remember how Katya suddenly appeared in our back yard and wouldn't go away? We checked all around the neighborhood, but no one knew anything about her. A beautiful Russian Blue like Katya doesn't just show up out of nowhere. At the time, I felt an energy from a caring being of some kind—one that seemed specifically oriented to animals—encouraging her to come to us. Once we took her in, I imagined this animal-protecting Angel smiling, knowing that the cat would be safe and loved here. Didn't you feel any of that, Dad?"

"Nope, but I do remember how excited you and your mom were. When I got home, all I noticed was this big silver cat acting as though she owned the place, and both of you spoiling her rotten."

Sara chimed in, "Tom, you know very well that you were smitten with Katya as soon as you set eyes on her."

"Well, I'll admit she was pretty special."

William had been listening curiously, enjoying the deep caring and love that were so evident in the easy interaction and light banter they had. His face clouded briefly as he remembered his own childhood that had been so lacking in any expression of love or appreciation.

When he returned to the present, it was with a deep joy and gratitude once again that he'd met this amazing person, and that she was willing to allow him into her life, to the point of meeting her parents. He reflected on what genuinely good people they were—no wonder Chantel was such a special girl!

The conversation continued amiably for a few hours. As William and Chantel got up to leave, Sara disappeared into the kitchen for a couple of minutes, returning with two bags full of dinner leftovers. "Thought you might enjoy having something on hand so you won't have to cook tomorrow," she said as she handed William and Chantel each a "goody bag."

After goodbyes and hugs all around, William and Chantel got into the car for their drive back to the city. Tom and Sara relaxed in the living room, sharing their approval of the young man courting their daughter. Outside, the Angel watching over their home smiled. Continuing her glad task of blessing and protecting the place, she filled it with luminous currents of warmth, peace, and joy.

Chapter 13
Upward Path

Hiking along the remote forest path, William and Chantel came upon a centuries-old oak. She squeezed his hand and gestured to the right.

"See that marker ahead, just beyond the little snowdrift? That's where the steeper side-trail begins. It's a rough climb, but worth it. There are absolutely fantastic views!"

"Is that the place you told me about before?"

"Yes, that's the one—I'd love to show it to you. Can we go there right now?"

With a smile, he responded, "Sure–let's do it!" They turned onto the path, which emerged suddenly from the shady vegetation to climb upward with many switchbacks along a barren rock face.

Since he'd met Chantel, his life had been filled with happy surprises. He'd long been conscientious and purposeful; now he had joy as well. Chantel's vibrant faith, optimism and spontaneity were a perfect complement to his seriousness and quiet determination.

He'd always been one to think things through, deliberating patiently and mulling over all aspects before reaching a decision. Chantel's choices, by contrast, were almost immediate. She'd ask herself a question, go silent just a moment, and then with a shining smile, say, "Yes, of course, that's the way it should be."

William would write long detailed lists of pros and cons. He'd weigh the alternatives, seek advice and counsel from experts, and eventually make a deliberate, logically satisfying decision. Chantel would formulate her question, and then wait for a flash of intuition or a signal. As she told William one day, "My heart tells me what to do."

This enchanted William. He couldn't help loving this girl who continually brought bright new ways of looking at things. Her appreciation of simple pleasures—softly falling snowflakes, the vivid green of shoots of grass, the random dancing path of a butterfly, the unique notes of birdsong—was contagious.

Her joy in music, and her ability to clearly convey specifics about its nuances, also intrigued William. He'd always liked music, humming when he was happy, but basically knew nothing about it. Country Western was different from Classical symphonies—that's as far as he got.

Chantel's musical expertise came from extensive knowledge as well as intuition. Whenever William asked Chantel about a piece that made him feel good, she'd be able to explain the feelings of the composer, the subtlety of choosing a particular instrument or voice to convey this feeling, the reasons for playing it in a certain key or at a certain tempo. On occasion she'd overwhelm him with her knowledge, and he would interrupt in mock irritation: "Enough already! Information overload!"

She'd stop, then smilingly agree: "You're right—we don't need to know all the details. Let's just feel what the music brings."

Each engrossed in their own thoughts, they continued hiking. The trail became yet narrower and steeper, and they had to stop frequently to catch their breath.

Chantel deeply appreciated William's depth and steadfastness. William was utterly trustworthy—an archetypal friend. Her heart told her that no matter what difficulties or dangers might lie ahead, nothing could harm her if he was nearby.

In some ways William reminded her of her father, who was always dependable and supportive. But although her father loved her a lot, he could never understand her. She'd tried, over and over again, to explain her experiences, but he would just chuckle and say, "I have no idea what you're talking about, sweetie, but if it makes you happy, that's the most important thing." And then he'd give her a "Don't worry, everything will be fine" hug.

On the trail now she realized once again how *right* it felt to be with William, how totally natural. It truly was like being reunited with her dearest friend; one she'd known in the far past. She smiled at that impression—what if it was true?

William had planned to propose to Chantel today, thinking that since she loved nature so much, this forest and its protecting mountain would provide the perfect setting. He'd written his lists, deeply pondered the choices, and thought he'd reached an irrevocable conclusion. But the doubts surfaced now, magnifying with every step. What if she didn't reciprocate his feelings? What if she didn't want to be more than friends? What if he'd been horribly mistaken about her feelings, and that she'd never want to see him again after his declaration of love?

"Is something wrong, William? Are you all right?"

"Um—just thinking," was his brief answer as he nervously fingered the small ring box in his pocket.

He continued mulling over his choices—should he get down on one knee? Should he have asked her father first? Should he wait for a more romantic setting? Should he have made a prepared speech? As to the ring—when he'd picked it out at the jewelry store, it seemed perfect, but what if she didn't like it?

Absorbed in his thoughts, he didn't notice how precipitous the trail had become. He slipped on a loose stone and skidded over the edge, accompanied by a smattering of pebbles and rocks. Below him was a straight rocky drop of perhaps 60 feet. Suddenly he felt hands across his back, firmly pushing him up and in, toward the mountain. He landed on his knees on a narrow ledge about four feet below the trail, unhurt but thoroughly coated with sand and debris. He turned his head to thank the person who had saved him, *but no one was there.* That couldn't be!

He had no time to ponder this mystery though, as

he struggled to get the last few feet back up onto the trail. Each time he reached a handhold it crumbled and fell away. He simply couldn't make it up alone.

All at once he laughed, seeing just how dense he'd been. It had taken a tumble off the trail and a strong shove from an unseen presence to knock some sense into him. He was filled with sudden joy at the realization of, "What better time than right now?"

Wiping his dusty hands on his jeans, and still on his knees, he pulled out the small box and offered it to her. "Chantel, I need your help to get back on the trail. And…I need your help in keeping on the upward path of life. Will you take my hand in friendship and love so we can take this path together always? Will you marry me?"

He looked upward into her face to see her reaction—a gasp, followed by the delighted look he had come to think of as "sparkles."

Without saying a word, but her eyes dancing, she took the box with one hand, then extended the other so he could pull himself up. They melted into a tight embrace, after which Chantel said, "Of course I'll marry you! But it won't be just you helping me. It's going to be an equal partnership, with both of us helping each other, no matter what life brings. I'd like nothing better than to spend a lifetime with you.

"Now, as to this little box, will you do the honors? I can hardly wait to see what's inside!"

He opened the ring box, revealing within the velvet lining a simple golden circlet designed with two hearts surrounding a modest but flawless diamond.

Chantel looked at it, then turned her face away.

"Don't you like it?" he asked anxiously. Sighing deeply, he continued, "I am so dumb—should have let you pick out the ring."

Chantel looked directly at him. "William, sweetheart, stop for a minute. The reason I turned away was so you wouldn't see me crying with joy. This ring is more beautiful than I could ever have imagined: it will be a perfect symbol of our love through the years."

Fighting a momentary lump in his throat, William brushed away her tears. After a moment, he deflected the emotion with a casual, "Whew—you had me worried there for a minute. Now that that's settled, let's see if it fits."

With a smile, she extended her left hand. He placed the ring on her finger, where it fit as though it had always been there. Its brilliance reflected Chantel's "sparkles" as the two of them continued to the mountain vantage point.

On arriving, they sat on a level boulder that overlooked a densely forested valley and had glorious vistas of snow-covered mountain ranges in the distance. The murmuring breeze carried scents of fresh water and of cool green leaves, bringing them refreshment and renewal.

After a few moments of gazing in silence at the panorama before them, they began to share some of their visions for the future, and of their aspirations and ideals for marriage.

William opened with his vision for an animal sanctuary. "Remember when we first met, Chantel? When I told you I heard a voice telling me about my Real Work?" She nodded.

"Well, now I know what it's going to be. The other day someone brought in two emaciated and abused animals. They'd just been tossed out on the roadside and left to die. My heart nearly broke at seeing them. Suddenly I heard the voice again, '*This* will be your Work—to provide a home for creatures like these. Give them a sanctuary in nature where they'll always be safe, cared for and loved.' So, I'll be looking for a place to build that sanctuary."

"A nature sanctuary, William? How wonderful! It will surely be a place of healing for animals, and those people who help them will be blessed in working with them."

Chantel then softly shared her own dreams of introducing young people to a pristine location in nature, guiding them in expanding their awareness and increasing their sensitivity to the harmonies of life all around.

"Really? You want to do that?"

"Yes, I've been writing about these hopes and dreams in my journal for years."

"Chantel, this is so perfect. The sanctuary will be ideal for both purposes!"

Their eyes met in renewed wonder. Could this really be?

As they continued talking, they found that when one of them began a sentence, the other would often pick up the thought and complete it. Delighted at this understanding and agreement, they made the beginnings of the sentences progressively shorter. What had begun as "I've always dreamed of a house in the country, surrounded by…" soon became, "It would be great if we could live…" and by the end of the afternoon shrank to "Let's…" The conversation had begun on a serious note, but by this time Chantel and William were laughing so hard it didn't matter how the sentences were completed!

They'd stayed on the mountain longer than planned, so it was nearly dark by the time they reached the car. The drive to Chantel's apartment was comfortably relaxed as they continued sharing the dreams of their hearts and souls.

Instead of running right in, Chantel offered, "How about a bite to eat—you're probably starving! It'll take me just a few minutes to fix us something. Why don't you pick out a CD so we can listen during dinner?"

True to her word, Chantel put together a quick and simple but delicious meal. They held hands while saying grace. (William had adopted that custom soon after observing it at Chantel's parents' home and now couldn't imagine eating a meal without giving thanks. And at this moment he was more thankful than he'd *ever* been in his life!)

Later that evening, after they kissed goodnight, the last thing he said to Chantel before driving back to his own place was, "What an amazing day! I still can't believe it!"

To himself he added, "And it's only the beginning of an even more amazing life! She loves me!" On the way home, William found himself humming what he called "Chantel's Song," the haunting melody the two of them had shared way back when they were first getting acquainted.

Back in her apartment, Chantel was singing the

very same piece. Words for a new verse came to her. She smiled as she wrote down:

> *God's blessed us so, my dearest one,*
> *With joy beyond compare.*
> *And growth toward Light we've now begun*
> *In unity to share.*

Chapter 14
The Wedding

Back when they'd first gotten engaged, William and Chantel had visited her folks to share their good news. After the initial hugs and congratulations, Sara had asked about their specific plans.

Chantel responded, "We'd like the wedding ceremony to be very simple and small, in the church this May, with Pastor White officiating."

William added, "Early afternoon is probably best. The sun will be shining through the stained glass behind the altar then."

Her eyes dancing, Chantel continued, "It would be wonderful to have spring wildflowers for the bouquets—we both love nature so much. If you and Dad want a big reception, that's fine. But please, Mom, just family and close friends for the wedding itself."

Sara asked, "Do you know yet who you'd like for your attendants?"

William spoke firmly. "Joe will be my Best Man."

Chantel said, "And Kerrie has to be the Matron of Honor—can't imagine anyone else!"

Mrs. Wyler's face lit up at the mention of Kerrie. "What would you think of asking Kerrie's twins to be the ring-bearer and flower girl?"

"Oh Mom, that would be perfect!" Nate and Kate were four years old. Chantel was their godmother; she loved them both dearly. They in turn adored their "Auntie Chantel."

Sara nodded. "Now, what can we do to help you with all this?"

William answered, "We don't want to impose on you, but would you be willing to check out reception venues? Chantel and I have such crazy work schedules that we haven't been able to do that yet."

"Of course, I'd love to," replied Sara, as Tom nodded in agreement. "For the reception, do you want just cake and punch, or light snacks, or should this be a formal dinner?"

"We want the guests to be relaxed and happy, Mom. Whatever you decide will be fine."

"OK, honey," she replied. "I'll start calling around for places for the reception. It's going to be such fun doing this!"

Chantel's parents began their research right away. Scheduling the wedding at the church was a snap, but as far as arranging the reception, things didn't work out so well. They went to several venues in the area: big halls, formal gardens, country clubs, even golf courses. Those that would have been appropriate were either booked up or were far too expensive. They even checked out the old Caslan house, which someone had bought and restored to its original Victorian beauty. This entire property had now been transformed into an upscale, gracious event locale—the Caslan Centre—complete with arched pathways leading to formal gardens, a charming gazebo, and restoration of its original 19th century grandeur. When they mentioned this possibility to the young couple, though, William stiffened.

His voice was flat and cold. "No, it can't be there."

The moment her folks left, Chantel's concern came through as she asked, "What was that all about? When the Caslan Centre came up, you looked like you'd seen a ghost."

With a bleak expression he responded, "Chantel, when your folks mentioned that place, it brought back memories of something I did there a long time ago that was very wrong."

She stroked his cheek gently. "Would it help if you told me more?"

Stumbling over his words, he haltingly confessed to her his childhood trespass into the Caslan house on that long-ago stormy night.

"William, you were just a kid. You followed orders from a boy who knew what he was doing was wrong, but I sense that you yourself were simply hoping to be accepted, to have friends. You didn't have any of those when you were growing up.

"From what you've told me before, your Mom was never there for emotional support. In my counseling I've found, over and over, that people need to have someone who cares. Kids will do almost anything to get that."

William protested: "Even though I was young, I should have known better. It's…I'm so ashamed…I've never been able to forget that night."

"Is there anything else you remember after the storm was over? Something from later that night?"

He was silent for a few minutes, trying to recall that long-ago time. Slowly, a smile began to play on his face. "Oh, yeah—now I remember. When Hooshee and I got home, I cleaned him up and dried him off. Later, he slept on the rug by my bed. I kept my hand on his fur because it felt so warm and soft. That touch comforted and soothed me all night long."

Chantel squeezed his hand. "Hooshee was a better friend than those kids would ever be."

"He sure was—I couldn't have made it without him."

"Thank you for sharing your experience with me," she continued. "I understand why you wouldn't want the reception there, and agree totally. Our wedding celebration shouldn't have any tinge of darkness or regrets."

She smiled, the familiar sparkles returning to her face. "Don't worry, William. The right place is out there—you'll see."

A few weeks later, on her morning walk, Sara encountered the Bransons, the elderly couple who owned the 50-acre parcel behind the Wyler home. The stream and trees that Chantel had played in so long ago formed the border between the two properties. The Bransons were strolling along cautiously, slowly, taking what they called their "morning constitutional."

"What a treat to see you again," Sara greeted them. "How have you been?"

Gesturing to their property with his cane, Mr. Branson said, "We're fine, but can't get back here as often as we'd like—it's a mighty long drive. So, tell us what's happening in your lives. How is that sweet little daughter of yours? She must be almost grown up by now."

Sara chuckled. "All grown up—got her master's degree three years ago and works as a school counselor and voice teacher. She recently got engaged to a fine young man, a veterinarian."

At this point Mrs. Branson squealed, "I can't believe it—little Carol Ellen is getting married? Have they set the date and the place yet?"

Sara answered, "Yes, they're having a small private ceremony in Pastor White's church the second Saturday in May. But we haven't found a site for the reception yet. Both of them really love nature, so we're hoping to find an outdoor location. We'd considered having it in our back yard, but that's way too small."

She added with genuine enthusiasm, "We'd love to have you come to the reception, wherever it ends up."

The Bransons looked at each other in brief wordless communication. With a slight nod to her husband, Mrs. Branson asked, "Would you consider having the reception across the creek on our place? You could use your house as a staging area for decorations and food, and have the guests gather in our meadow."

"Wha...I think that would be perfect! Before I mention it to Sara and William, though, are you sure you'd be willing to do this?"

Mr. Branson said, "Of course—and we'll have the meadow mowed for you in time for the wedding. But there's a problem with getting over there to set things up." He thought a moment, then asked, "Remember the old wooden bridge that used to cross the stream?"

Looking puzzled, Sara replied: "Of course, but that bridge washed away before our daughter was even born."

Branson continued, "I imagine the footings are still there—concrete, you know. What would you think about having it rebuilt in time for the wedding? We could pay for the materials...that would be our wedding gift."

Mrs. Branson added, "And it would help bring us all closer together again. We've really missed being here. Did you know, Sara, that my grandparents originally came out here as pioneers and homesteaded this whole section—one square mile—of land?"

"Had no idea—I'd love to hear more about that! Maybe you can come over for dinner this summer and tell us about your grandparents and the history of this area."

They agreed on a date, then went their separate ways.

Continuing on her walk, Sara gradually became aware that she'd been humming. She chuckled to note that it was "The Hills are Alive" from *Sound of Music*. She'd check with Chantel and William, of course, but as far as Sara was concerned, this offer was a godsend.

That evening she told William and Chantel about the morning conversation, and asked how they felt about a reception in the meadow across the creek. William took a moment to analyze logistics and other possible issues with the site. "That would be really nice, out in nature yet very accessible. Can't imagine a better place to share this happy time."

Chantel broke into a radiant smile, followed by, "Oh Mom, it's perfect, perfect, perfect!"

After a moment, William diffidently suggested, "If it's OK with him, Tom and I could build the bridge together on weekends."

Tom readily agreed and within a few days the men drew up plans and got the materials for the bridge, starting construction the following weekend. Tom and William worked together well, sometimes talking but more often in companionable silence. While building the solid bridge to cross the stream, they found themselves creating another one as well—this one to connect their lives with respect and understanding.

※ ※ ※

"Somebody grab the phone, please!" shouted Sara. Not normally one to raise her voice, she was at the other end of the house adding the finishing touches to the outfits that Nate and Kate would wear. Regardless of whether it was the florist, caterer, or someone else involved in the wedding festivities, she knew the call was important and had to be answered.

Tom amiably picked up: "Hello—Wyler

residence." Within thirty seconds, though, he was shaking his head in bewilderment. "Wait just a minute, I'll put my wife on the line."

"Honey, it's the florist. They need to know something about…fillup flowers?"

"Filler flowers, dear. Tell them I'll be right there."

Chantel had stopped by her parents' house on the way to a counseling session with one of her students. It was time to leave, but she couldn't help chuckling at the overheard conversation. She'd already said goodbye to her mother, and heading out the door, gave her father a big hug. "Thanks, Dad. You're the greatest!"

"Never knew a wedding could be this complicated. What're filler flowers, anyway?"

She glanced at her watch, responding, "Better let Mom explain: I mustn't be late for my appointment. Bye—love you!"

Despite the myriad wedding ideas, planning and preparations swirling all around her, Chantel herself remained serene and centered. She was happy seeing her mother throwing herself so enthusiastically into coordinating the plans, and since their tastes were very much the same, had confidence in her decisions. As far as Dad was concerned, his wife and daughter were speaking a foreign language when they discussed plans. Even though he had no idea of the details involved, he was being a good sport about the whole thing.

The last few weeks had flown by in a whirl of activity: it seemed as though the wedding rehearsal was upon them in no time. Tom was amazed that everything fell into place so well. At the dinner afterwards, he and

Sara held hands, smiling at each other and remembering their own wedding long ago as well as the joys that the following years had brought.

The following day, the chapel was transformed into a woodland glade for the wedding. Wildflowers and willow branches adorned the altar and the ends of the pews, which were gradually filling with family and close friends. A moss-green runner made the center aisle a forest path for the bride's entrance. Sunshine streamed through the stained-glass windows. A folk harp playing softly in the background evoked hints of birdcalls, breezes and running water.

The ceremony itself began with organ pipes ringing out a wedding processional, an original piece composed by Chantel's favorite professor from college.

Kerrie, resembling a graceful forest goddess in spring green satin, glided serenely toward the altar. Her sunny smile was due in equal parts to happiness for Chantel and to memories of her own wedding.

Little Nate, in white suit with green cummerbund and tie, began to walk down the aisle. He took his responsibilities very seriously. Kerrie had explained about what would happen at the wedding ceremony, including the phrase "With this ring I thee wed." With brow furrowed intently, he kept his eyes on the rings the whole time, almost losing his footing as he wove back and forth along the aisle because he was concentrating so hard.

Kate wore a delicate light green dress with darker green sash. Carrying a flower basket, she tossed the contents enthusiastically on and around the aisle, covering people nearby with petals.

The guests couldn't help but smile at seeing the children performing their duties in such a delightful manner.

A brief pause, then everyone rose as Chantel and her father stepped onto the carpet. Tom beamed proudly. Chantel, radiant in a simple yet elegant wedding gown and carrying a woodland bouquet, seemed almost to float down the aisle.

The ceremony itself was brief, reverent, and simple. After Chantel and William had recited their vows and the rings were exchanged, they clasped hands and jointly shared another promise for all to hear:

We will walk together, hand in hand

Full partners on the path of life

Wherever it may lead us

Aspiring toward the Mountaintop—

The Glory of God.

They then turned back to the minister for his prayer and blessing. As he concluded with, "...I now pronounce you husband and wife," a sudden brilliant outpouring of light appeared above the altar. Created by the great Angel presiding in the church and joined by the Guardian Angels of Chantel and William, this light swirled down to envelop them, uniting and sealing them in its benediction of pure Love.

Although both the minister and the wedding couple felt the sudden rush of Power and knew that something very special had happened, only the children saw its source. They both burst into radiant smiles. Nate stayed silent, although his eyes were huge and his mouth opened in a surprised "O" of awe on seeing the outshining of the Angels. Kate whispered, "Look! Look! Beautiful sparkles!"

Several young choir members then burst into the joyful "Alleluia" from *Sound of Music* for the wedding party recessional. Hand in hand, the beaming newlyweds made their way quickly out of the church and drove to an unlikely location, special to both of them.

Unusual but not really surprising, this was the veterinary office. Their very first congratulations came from the resident office cat, Tux, who purred and ecstatically wrapped himself around their ankles.

Petting Tux while trying to remove black cat hair from her wedding dress, Chantel asked, "Is this the way our life will always be?" At the same instant, William said, "Is this a portent?" That set them off into gales of laughter that continued as they prepared for the formal wedding photographs.

A short time later, William and Chantel arrived at her parents' home. As William, with a flourish, escorted his bride across the newly built bridge to the meadow, the guests burst into spontaneous applause. Food had been set up buffet-style and the area was dotted with picnic tables and benches. The flow was straightforward: well-wishers greeted the wedding party, filled their plates, and sat wherever they liked.

Toasts were funny and short: then the music started up and dancing began. Kids scampered around playing games or giggling; grownups talked, laughed, and danced, while the oldest guests smiled benevolently at the flurry of activities.

By the wall near the old willow tree, Shana and Griff, the nature beings who had been Chantel's childhood friends, smiled too.

"Look at her now, Griff—all grown up."

"Yes, she's become a beautiful young lady. And the younger man who was building the bridge—what do they call him—William? Anyhow, he and Carol Ellen genuinely love each other—just look at their auras."

"Do you suppose she remembers us?"

"I hope so, but humans are funny that way—most of them forget all about us when they grow up."

"Do you think they'll find our gifts?"

After the guests had all left, Chantel and William started back across the bridge. Suddenly they stopped, looking closely at the willow tree. There, a little above head height, several branches had grown into a clear set of intertwined hearts. Chantel breathed, "It's beautiful! That has to be from Shana and Griff."

Stepping closer to the tree, William gazed down to see a sparkling white, unmistakably heart-shaped stone near the trunk.

"Look—this must be from them too." He picked it up and presented it to Chantel.

She called out quietly, "Shana…Griff…Thank you for your special gifts—we'll treasure them always."

The nature beings were thrilled that their presents had been received and appreciated. They added their unique nature blessing to the happy newlyweds, who felt it as a caress of the breeze. For an instant, Chantel saw two shimmering faces—the same dear companions she remembered from her childhood, a bit larger and older but unmistakably Shana and Griff. At the same time,

William heard peals of delightfully contagious laughter within the rustling of the leaves.

Chantel turned to William. "Did you see them? They were both right over there."

He chuckled, "Didn't see a thing, but oh how they laughed—such joy!"

Sharing their perceptions of the experience as they walked hand in hand toward the house, they agreed that what the nature beings had given them was the loveliest of all the presents they'd received.

"From their hearts to ours," William said.

Chantel added, "Remember the Minister quoting Corinthians: *and the greatest of these is Love?* This stone will be a talisman to remind us of the gift of Love, every day."

And so began their married life.

Chapter 15
Ideals, Dreams, Openings

Chantel and William plopped down on the couch, exhausted. They'd just gotten home from another arduous day seeking property that might work for their dreamed-of animal sanctuary. They'd begun several months ago by searching in a 25-mile radius, and with each trip, they expanded the range by several miles. The next step would involve extending this to adjacent states, hoping for something better elsewhere.

William couldn't help being discouraged. "Honey, maybe we're not supposed to do this. I'm happy with being a veterinarian here in town. The pets and their owners like me. It's a rewarding and secure profession."

He put his arm around her, continuing, "And look at you—you're a great counselor, your music students adore you, and you're getting lots of opportunities to sing."

Chantel responded, "Of course—this is a

wonderful life. You're a terrific vet, darling, and I do love sharing music with people. We've been really blessed. But are you saying that we should give up the idea of an animal sanctuary? That this whole thing is just a pipe dream? Why would God have put this idea into our hearts if He knew it wouldn't be doable?"

William was silent for a moment. "I don't know. Maybe it's some sort of a test He set up? We've looked everywhere and keep hitting brick walls. What if He's saying, "Forget it"?

"We know God wants the best for us, and has a plan for us, one that's far better than we can even imagine. There'll be a sign—all we have to do is be open to His guidance!"

William nodded agreement, once again marveling at this incredible blessing in his life, the remarkable loving companion he'd married three years ago.

They sat quietly on the couch for a while, just appreciating each other's nearness. Then, as if on cue, they both yawned hugely.

Chantel's laugh bubbled up, "That was perfect timing—race you to bed!"

※ ※ ※

At breakfast next morning, Chantel said, "Last night I had the most vivid dream. We were in our sanctuary, and it was *right here*. You were in your office treating the animals, but at the same time it was out in nature and you were working with healing energies—they looked like scintillating balls of light. There were all sorts of animals there—not just dogs and cats, but zebras, lions, chickens, even a unicorn! I was teaching the kids from our school, and when we were all singing under the huge trees, I could hear the trees singing with us. Everything was morphed into a huge glowing experience of unity—I don't know any other way to express it. It felt so real!"

William replied, "That's beautiful—hope you'll put that one in your journal."

"Yes, after that dream, I'm even more certain that there is a place being prepared for us. Do you suppose it's something that's so obvious that we're missing it—like right under our noses?"

"Hmmm, could be. I had a dream too, but…" Glancing at his watch, he changed to, "Gotta go. The morning is scheduled with back-to-back surgeries!"

They hugged and kissed goodbye, with a final "I love you," before William headed off to his veterinarian practice.

Driving to work, William mulled over his own dream, actually relieved that there hadn't been time to describe it to Chantel right away. Compared to hers, his had been much stranger and more complex.

As was his long-time habit, he was the first one at the office. Arriving early gave him precious time to envision the day ahead. Once there, he began dictating his dream on his tape recorder:

In the dream, I was in the center of a gray stone spiral path on a bright spring day. I began to walk the spiral, taking one step, then another and another—what seemed like a journey of hundreds of miles. As I circled out, the landscape gradually became obscured by a cold, penetrating mist that got steadily denser and darker. By the time I reached the farthest point of the spiral, there was no light at all. I was shivering from the dank coldness that seemed to be sucking out all my body heat and my vital energy as well. I could see nothing, but sensed a desolate plain with a huge abyss ahead. A phrase from Dante's Inferno came to me: "Abandon all hope, you who enter here."

A voice, as sharp and piercing as the icy surroundings, whispered. "Go back—you don't belong here. This is not what you're searching for. Go back, go back, go back!"

"It's too cold, too dark; I'll get lost. I can't do it."

"You must!" The whisper lost none of its sternness but was slightly less harsh. "Turn around and return the way you came. Your destiny is in the Center with Light, not here frozen at the Edge of Darkness."

"But... I... can't... move!"

"Yes, you can." After a long silence, as though considering whether to say more, the voice slowly and deliberately continued, "Now go, before it's too late. Help will come when you need it."

I turned in despair, every muscle aching with cold. As there was no way of seeing the path, I felt my way one cautious step at a time. Utterly exhausted, I stumbled several times, but kept on going. After an interminable period, the blackness began to lift. The atmosphere was still a heavy dark gray, but I could now see the stones and the curving way a few feet ahead of me.

Continuing slowly, I realized that I'd stopped shivering. Visibility was improving, and there was a hint of blue to the thinning gray mist. I stood straighter, now determined to keep on going to make it back to the starting point.

After another long while, I saw bits of green—tufts of grass growing beyond the ever-present rocks, and what appeared to be trees in the mist. And now there was distant birdsong—the most life-affirming sound I'd ever heard. I smiled and opened my arms wide, almost dancing as I approached the center.

On reaching the center of the spiral, which had become a meadow, I was filled with a steadfast "rightness." This feeling persisted even after I woke up.

Still dictating, William asked himself, OK, what does this mean in terms of my life? Why did I take the path that spun me out into that horrible experience of cold emptiness? Why was I able to return to the center? And just what is the center? Exterior circumstances? Something inside me? Why did it seem so "right"?

He put the dream assessment aside as he prepared for the day ahead. First he reviewed the charts for his morning surgery schedule, silently blessing each of the animals and sending them waves of calmness. Many of the procedures were routine, but one was going to be very complex. Courage, his friend Joe's special companion dog, had developed a tumor, one so large it was pressing against vital organs. Surgery to remove the tumor would be extremely risky, beyond William's expertise as a general practice veterinarian. William had explained this to Joe and had recommended that a specialist perform the surgery.

Joe had flatly refused, with "No way am I going to send him to a stranger that doesn't know him. I trust you. Courage trusts you. If you can't do this, nobody can."

So this morning, William carefully studied Courage's lab results, ultrasound, X-rays, and every page of the chart from the first time he'd seen the dog. William had long ago found that, just as with human patients, an animal's recovery often depended on its will to live. He once again evaluated Courage's general health condition and his personality. Courage was wise, loyal, patient and utterly dedicated to Joe. If the dog survived the operation, these traits would certainly help him pull through.

He performed the routine surgeries on all his other patients first, in order to allow ample time to deal with whatever he might encounter in Courage's operation. Finally he began to work on Courage. After the abdomen was opened, he saw that things were even more difficult than he'd imagined. The tumor was pressing on vital organs and entwined around the aorta. He truly didn't know what to do: any steps he might take were life-threatening. Reluctantly, he even considered the idea of increasing the anesthesia so that Courage would pass on the operating table rather than have to suffer prolonged agony with an ever-growing tumor.

While documenting the dog's vital signs at 11:30, he suddenly became aware of a Presence in the operating room, one that was broadcasting healing, wisdom, and peace. William received a flash of insight. He "saw" as though on a screen before him, a totally new and safe approach to the surgery. Following these new directions, his hand guiding the scalpel was sure and swift. The tumor was removed almost effortlessly. Before checking the status of everything else in the dog's abdominal cavity, he breathed a silent prayer of thanks for the guidance he'd received. Perfect—no invasion, no damage; everything looked normal. The tumor curling around the aorta had been large enough to impair circulation. Now that it was removed, William smiled at how steadily and regularly that huge blood vessel beat. No more problems there! As he prepared samples of tissue for lab analysis, he once again received the inner assurance: "Courage will be all right. This is benign."

Later that afternoon, William phoned Joe to report the condition of Courage.

William said, "Hi, I'm calling to give you an update on Courage. He's…"

In a rush of words, Joe interrupted: "Let me tell you, I was pretty worried at first, even though I was praying for him all morning. But then all at once the stress lifted. I was totally at peace—I *knew* that Courage would be healed. After that, there was never any doubt."

"Do you remember what time that was, Joe?"

"Sure—it was exactly 11:30. Why do you ask?"

"First, Joe, let me tell you that you're absolutely right. Courage came through the surgery with flying colors.

"Second, this is the toughest surgery I've ever done. The tumor was wrapped around his aorta and was pushing against his pancreas and spleen. There was no way it could be removed—totally inoperable. It was an impossible situation, and I was about to—well, I was about to give up. But then Someone appeared, showing me exactly how to resolve this insoluble problem. He guided me through all the necessary steps. Can you guess what time that was?"

As the realization sank in, Joe answered, "11:30,

right?"

William's voice broke slightly as he responded, "Precisely." Regaining control of his emotions, he reverted to his professional mode: "The tumor was removed, there was no damage to the internal organs, and Courage is resting in the recovery area. You can pick him up any time after five tonight."

When Joe arrived later that evening, Courage thumped his tail happily to see his master. William gave Joe verbal and written instructions for post-operative care of the dog. Joe acknowledged that he understood what to do, then went silent. With eye contact, a firm handclasp, and a mutual, heartfelt "Thank you" that expressed volumes, their communication was complete. No further words were needed.

Giving Courage a final pat on the head, William handed him over to Joe.

On his way home, William wondered again about the strange dream he'd had. Perhaps it had to do with the decisions in his treatment of Courage...but no, that didn't feel right.

He scarcely got the door open before Chantel, even more bubbly than usual, welcomed him with a huge hug and kiss.

Without waiting to ask him how his day went, her words raced out breathlessly, almost one on top of another. "Honey, Mom phoned me a few minutes ago with incredible news. The Bransons have decided to sell their land, and they're offering it to our family first."

"Whoa—slow down! Say that all over again, please."

She repeated what she'd said, then continued without a pause, "They're willing to sell it to us below market price because they know how much we love it and that we would keep it natural and pristine."

William was dumbfounded. "Wait a minute—this can't be. Do you mean…?"

"Yes—that could be our animal sanctuary!"

He shook his head in disbelief: "After the time and effort we've spent searching all over…and it could be right here? Are you sure the Bransons are committed to selling?"

"Absolutely! They came over to talk to Mom and Dad today. They even hinted that it could be done as an easy border adjustment, since the properties are adjoining, and the bridge that you and Dad built forms a preexisting connection."

William responded, "That's amazing—there's no place anywhere that would be more ideal for our animal sanctuary. How large is the parcel?"

"I believe Mom said it's 50 acres, but we'd have to check that."

A shadow came over his face. "C'mon, Chantel, sweetie, be realistic. We've put aside some money, but no way we can afford a 50-acre chunk of land! It's impossible!"

Chantel's enthusiasm wasn't at all dampened. "Nothing's impossible for God—but we certainly don't have to decide right this minute. Let's let the idea incubate for a while."

She sat on the couch, gesturing for him to join her. They sat quietly for a few minutes, lost in their own thoughts as they reviewed the events of the day.

Chantel broke the silence: "This morning you mentioned a dream that you were going to tell me about later. Is now a good time?"

"Sure—why not," he answered and proceeded to describe it to her in as much detail as he remembered. Finishing, he shivered, "It was so cold...so dark and empty out there. I'll never forget that...but then getting back to the center was like coming alive again, with warmth and beauty and song. Just like coming home to you, sweetheart. Haven't figured out what it means, though."

She smiled knowingly. "You will, honey, you will."

Chantel's mother invited the Bransons over for tea the next Saturday, and asked William and Chantel to join them to discuss the land sale further.

After a period of polite small talk, Mr. Branson asked, "Have you given any more thought to buying our land?"

Chantel's father answered. In what he hoped was a noncommittal tone, he said, "We've had some discussions. Why is it that you want to sell?"

Mrs. Branson looked at her husband for permission before replying. "We're not as young as we used to be, and, well, we've decided to move into a retirement community."

Chantel's mom murmured sympathetically to Mrs. Branson, "That must have been a tough choice, after living by yourselves for so long."

"It's not so hard. This place will give us freedom to live independently as long as we can, but when we need care, that'll be included too. And we have friends who live there."

Tom got back on topic: "Have you gotten a market appraisal yet?"

Mr. Branson answered: "We've talked to two realtors to find out an offering price. Would you like to see those papers?"

"Yes, please—that would let us know if there's even a possibility of considering this."

Mr. Branson placed the papers on the table. After the family studied them solemnly, Tom shook his head, saying, "I'm sorry, but we just don't have that much money."

Mrs. Branson said, "We thought that might be too high for you. Well, a little bird told us that William and Chantel have been wanting to create a sanctuary for abused, abandoned animals. In our younger days Mr. Branson and I dreamed of that too, but never were able to do it." On the verge of tears, she continued, "That's been one of the biggest regrets of our lives."

Mr. Branson took over for his wife. "We talked it over last night and want to offer the place to you for half the appraised value—but only if your daughter and son-in-law are willing to turn it into an animal sanctuary. We'd be honored to help in this way."

William, in a sudden flash, realized the meaning of his dream. He whispered his explanation to Chantel, recounting how it clearly ended with him being guided to a beautiful meadow.

Her face lit up like sunshine. "That's it—that's it exactly!"

The others looked on in bewilderment. Chantel explained: "The other night after we came home after another long day looking for our animal reserve, each of us had a vivid dream. We couldn't understand quite what the dreams meant at the time, but knew they were significant. With what you just said right now, their meaning became crystal clear."

She continued, "Would you excuse us for a moment while we talk this over with my parents?"

"Of course: we'll just go sit in your garden."

The family council was unanimous—of course they would buy the place! They quickly agreed that Chantel and William would contribute the funds they'd saved up for this, and Chantel's folks would loan them the rest with a promise to repay within ten years. As simply as that, things were settled. They walked out to meet the Bransons, whose quizzical expressions were replaced by smiles as soon as they saw the beaming faces of the family.

Mr. Wyler shook Mr. Branson's hand firmly. "Sir, we would be delighted to buy your land under the conditions you've specified."

Branson responded: "Splendid! If you'd like, this could be handled as a border adjustment, since the properties are adjoining and were all part of one larger parcel many years ago. Shall I look into that?"

"By all means: that would be the simplest and most straightforward.", Mr. Wyler responded enthusiastically.

William and Chantel and her mom weren't nearly as formal. First they hugged Mrs. Branson, and Chantel planted a kiss on her cheek. As soon as Mr. Branson was free, he got the same treatment.

Together, Chantel and William said, "This is the answer to our dreams. You have no idea how grateful we are—thank you!"

Mrs. Branson smiled broadly. "I can tell you'd like to see your place, so go on over and check it out."

Chantel and William grinned. Together they dashed across the bridge, children at heart again. In the middle of the meadow, they grabbed hands and spun around in a mutual circle till they were both dizzy. Over and over they repeated, "This is the dream. This is the center. This is right, this is warm, this is *real*!"

From forest, stream, hillside and meadow, the nature beings joined in affirmation—the song that Chantel had first heard so many years ago in the mountains, and the one that William had known forever.

Chapter 16
IDEALS BECOME REALITY

Soon after they purchased the land, William and Chantel started a foundation for the purpose of creating and maintaining the future animal and nature sanctuary. They'd wanted to call it the St. Francis Center Foundation, but their friend Joe, who was also a board member, vetoed that idea.

"Nope—an overtly religious name like that would be an automatic turnoff to the OLC kids. Besides, it might drive away some donors as well.

"Why don't we each check out some people who've actually *lived* what we're trying to do here? Next time we get together we can share those insights."

William responded, "Great idea. Let's do it!"

A few weeks later they got together again. Chantel led off with, "Even though you're very familiar with the two people I've chosen, they seem to speak to the essence of what we want for the sanctuary."

She first gave a brief biography of the great naturalist John Muir, concluding with two of his quotations. First was "Keep close to nature's heart…and break clear away, once in a while, and climb a mountain or spend a week in the woods. Wash your spirit clean," followed by, "Everybody needs beauty as well as bread, places to play in and pray in, where nature may heal and give strength to body and soul."

Still hoping to also honor the name of St. Francis, Chantel recapped the saint's life, ending with one of his lesser-known quotes: "Not to hurt our humble brethren is our first duty to them, but to stop there is not enough. We have a higher mission to be of service to them wherever they require it."

William described two of several persons interested in animal welfare. One was St. Blaise, a 4th century physician and bishop known particularly for healing both people and animals. The animals would come to him on their own for assistance, and if he was praying, the animals would wait patiently, not wishing to disturb his prayers. When he moved to a cave to avoid persecution, the wild animals visited, and he healed any that were sick and wounded.

Another was St. Modestos, a Patriarch of Jerusalem in the 7th century, who was a healer of animals. William then handed out Modestos' moving Prayer for Animals, that dealt specifically with animals who are sick or in danger. William read aloud an excerpt from that prayer: "…grant compassion on the suffering animals, whose herd is being afflicted by the sickle of death. And not having any word besides bleating, and bitter and random noises, in Your mercy, take away their passion and suffering."

Joe had focused on St. Martin de Porres, a Peruvian saint known for his care for people (especially poor children) and animals. Joe quoted from a biography that stated, "Martin devoted himself passionately to taking care of others.... If men came to him, he took care of them, at times effecting instantaneous cures; if animals came to him, he gave no less attention. In the majority of cases, Martin did not go in search of animals. It seemed like instinct would bring wounded animals to his infirmary, where St. Martin would fix them up and allow them to rest in his room until they were cured. From dogs to cats to mice, turkeys and chickens, St. Martin was always welcomed warmly by the animals, as they greeted him with joy, as if grateful for his charity."

He continued, "St. Martin was noted for work on behalf of the poor, establishing a children's hospital. He also founded a residence for orphans and abandoned children in the city of Lima."

Joe added: "I've always liked what Edward Flanagan, the founder of Boys Town, said. 'Our young people are our greatest wealth. Give them a chance and they will give a good account of themselves.'"

After a lively discussion, the three of them narrowed the choices to St. Francis, St. Blaise, and St. Martin. They wanted to honor these individuals for their works. Due to Joe's earlier comments, though, they were still uneasy about using religious titles.

Eventually William suggested, "Why not just call it the Francis Blaise Martin Foundation? That's a solid, dignified-sounding name."

"And we'll be the only ones who know where it came from, and that it's honoring these special souls,"

Chantel's Song

added Chantel.

Joe chuckled. "Yeah, but if the kids ever find out, they'll probably nickname the place 'Saints' Acres.'"

"If so, it'll be their own idea. Nothing wrong with that!" responded William.

Chantel went to the refrigerator and pulled out a pitcher of her mom's special iced tea recipe. She filled their glasses, saying, "We're all agreed, then? Here's to the Francis Blaise Martin Foundation, and the sanctuary!"

The three friends enthusiastically clinked their glasses together, toasting the new endeavor.

※ ※ ※

With a combination of diligent fundraising and their personal savings, there was finally enough capital to begin preparation of the property. First priority would be fencing around the entire acreage, then kennels and storerooms for food and equipment.

One morning the local fencing contractor came to them: "I heard about what you're trying to do with this place. I've seen far too many mistreated pets when we're out doing jobs. If you'll give' em a good home here, I'll donate materials for whatever you need for fencing. Just let me know when, where and how much." When his crew learned of the project, they volunteered their labor as well.

While the fencing was being installed, Chantel and William marked off locations of the buildings they hoped to have someday. They carefully selected these sites in order to preserve the mature trees. As the couple felt that trees themselves had healing energies along with their shady canopies, they agreed that none were to be cut unless absolutely necessary.

This morning they'd finished the final measurements on the first set of kennels. As soon as the marker stakes were set, Joe and two of the teenaged boys he was mentoring began digging trenches for the foundations. These would be kennels, yes, but not ramshackle structures. They would be sturdy and attractive, spacious, and super-easy to clean. Best of all, they'd be adjacent to a grassy meadow so all the dogs could run and play during the daytime.

The second structure was to be a "feline condo" with hideaways and perches for cats, so they could each discover their own special spot for rest and healing. Future plans included corrals and stables for horses, along with huge open areas for them to run or graze.

For now, their office was located in Chantel's childhood bedroom, and any treatments and surgical procedures would be done in William's downtown practice. However, future plans for the sanctuary included a large multipurpose building—barnlike in exterior appearance in order to blend with the countryside. The interior would be designed to contain the foundation's offices, animal hospital facilities, and a classroom/meeting hall.

Together with Joe, they had brainstormed the role of Joe's OLC kids in this endeavor. They decided that the kids would initially visit and help only during daytime. Throughout the year the young people would be learning useful construction skills by working on the new buildings. When those were done, they'd be caring for and companioning the animals, doing whatever needed to be done for their care. Come summer, a few of those teens who would benefit most from the healing of total immersion in nature would set up tents and camp out for a week or so, learning, observing and helping.

William and Chantel, Joe and many dedicated volunteers spent countless hours preparing, constructing, getting everything ready for the first phase of the sanctuary. Now, months later, the fencing was up, the outbuildings were prepared for the animals—everything was ready for the official opening. Joe had been looking forward to this event but had been called away on an emergency.

Animal lovers from all over the county (many of them bringing their leashed pets) turned out for this occasion. The ribbon-cutting ceremony began with a grandiose speech by the Mayor: "Good morning, ladies and gentlemen. Thank you for coming to our fine city, the home of friendly people, healthy air, and benign industry. Since becoming Mayor I've brought in three new industries, five more parks, fixed potholes in our roads, and succeeded in revitalizing the downtown area. Now it's time to see what's happening out in the countryside. My staff is planning big improvements here as well— extension of sewer and gas lines to you folks, better roads with more safety features, even a quicker response time for emergency services. Part of my city's master plan is to keep some of these outlying areas rural. I am pleased to say that this use of the land fits in well with my master plan."

After many more self-promoting statements, he

finally cut the ribbon, with a flourish and a broad gesture in the direction of the meadow. "We bring you the long-awaited Francis Blaise Martin Sanctuary, which has been the dream of our own local veterinarian, William Farragut, his wife Chantel, who teaches music at Central High school, and Joe Fortis, a counselor for at-risk youth. This has been their plan and vision for many years.

"And now Dr. Farragut will say a few words—let's give him a big hand!"

William stepped up, a big brown indeterminate-breed dog close by his side. He took a deep breath, looking at the well-wishers all around. "It's wonderful to see so many friends here today—two-legged and four-legged both. This could not have happened without your support and prayers. Our shared vision is that this place shall be a place of healing and of wholeness. Here, animals that have been abandoned, injured, or abused will know that they are safe and will learn to trust again. Once they have become healed in body and in spirit, and have received basic behavioral training, they will be eligible for adoption to a 'forever' home. Moreover, they'll have a home here for life if that's what they need."

He paused, hand-signaling for the dog to sit. "This is Huck. He's been totally deaf since he was a puppy. His owner planned to train him as a hunting dog. The man thought that shooting a rifle within inches of the puppy would be a good way of getting him used to this. Instead, both eardrums were ruptured. Now he was obviously no good for hunting and couldn't hear verbal commands. So his owner confined him in a pen with no companionship, no freedom to run—just the necessities of food and water.

"One of our local animal lovers saw Huck locked

in the pen and asked to buy him. The owner's response was, 'Go ahead and take the useless mutt—good riddance.' For over a year she worked with Huck. She taught him to respond to hand signals and gave him much patient love and caring. In return, he became her faithful, loyal companion. When she had to move to a smaller apartment where pets are not allowed, she asked if we could find a place for Huck, 'where he can run and feel the wind in his hair.'"

William now turned to Chantel with a smile. Cradling an orange tabby in her arms, she stepped up to the mike and began speaking. "Tabitha here was caught in a steel jaw trap. When one of the local farmers brought her in, her leg was so badly mangled that my husband had to amputate it. Huck and Tabitha have been living together at my parents' home for several months now and are best buddies. Although some people may think of them as disabled or handicapped, or as members of two species that aren't supposed to get along, these two dear ones are simply companions who have fun together."

She continued, "This sanctuary isn't just about animals—it's about young people too. Our good friend Joe is dedicated to helping bring them to wholeness and will be spending lots of time here with some of them. He was planning to be here for this occasion, but a last-minute emergency kept him away."

Now a young man in a crisp police uniform stepped up confidently. "Since Joe couldn't make it, he asked me to say a few words in his place. My name is Mark, and I've been on the police force over in Hillsdale for about two years now. Some of you have expressed concerns about at-risk youth spending time here at the sanctuary. I'd like to tell you a story, if I may."

He paused a moment, smiled, and began, "Once upon a time there was a scrawny kid who'd been abandoned by his parents at age 12. He spent the next few years sleeping on couches of various friends, or on the streets. He drifted into alcohol and drug usage. The juvenile authorities routinely picked him up, then released him with no charges. The boy had no goals, no purpose, no future. One day he met a counselor named Joe. Joe saw promise in this rudderless kid, took him under his wing, patiently mentored him, gave him a moral compass—in short, helped him see his true potential. With Joe's steadfast help and encouragement, the boy eventually returned to school, graduated from college, applied for Police Academy, and…well, here I am. I turned out OK."

The audience burst out in cheers and spontaneous applause for Mark.

Next, Chantel gently handed Tabitha over to Mark, taking the mic, and sang "Bless the Beasts and the Children." After the final notes rang out over the meadow, she said, "Welcome to the Francis Blaise Martin Sanctuary, Huck and Tabitha. May you and all your friends to follow know only joy, safety and love here."

With that, William and Mark released the animals into the meadow. The onlookers watched in delight as the dog and cat began exploring the terrain together. They romped on the grass, played with invisible companions, ran around to the fence lines, sniffed and explored to their heart's content. Finally they both fell asleep, with Tabitha curled up between Huck's paws.

While the animals were frolicking, the air had

been totally still, but once they settled down, the breezes came, making patterns in the grass that resembled visible traces of invisible dancers. In the forest beyond, the trees seemed to join the dance, their leaves rustling in a soft melody.

Then began a flurry of congratulations and well-wishes. All the while graciously interacting with the attendees, Chantel, just for an instant, saw heart-shaped pink glowing forms above the animals and a myriad of darting rainbow-hued sparkles throughout the meadow.

During this time, William heard a deep resonant tone that communicated peaceful benediction. Although he didn't actually see them, he got a distinct impression of numerous tall, beautiful Beings of Light smiling gently, their hands raised in blessing. They reminded him of the night he got his childhood dog, Hooshee, and of the bright Being of Light that was present then.

Chantel and William touched hands, silently communicating acknowledgement that each of them had been aware of something unusual.

※ ※ ※

A few hours later, after all the attendees had left, William and Chantel crossed the bridge to her parents' place to relax a little before heading home.

Chantel looked around for Tom. "Dad's not here? Is he OK?"

Sara responded, "He should be back pretty soon. He swears he can find blackberries in the forest now. Since he knows how much I like them he grabbed a couple of buckets and headed over there right after lunch to get us some."

Chantel smiled, "That's just like Dad—generous and thoughtful!" After a short pause she continued, "Do you think we should share some of our *inner* impressions from the dedication now, while he's still out there? We don't want to make him uncomfortable with stuff that he feels is 'too woo-woo.'"

"That's probably a good idea, honey. Your father is a wonderful man with a huge heart, and he loves us all immensely, as you know. But he does think we're a little bit nuts when we go on about things beyond the physical senses."

"He's certainly not the only one," William said. "Many of my colleagues are stuck in the paradigm of 'the physical world is the only reality.' No point in arguing with them. As far as they're concerned, if they can see, hear, smell, touch or taste something, it's real; otherwise it's not."

Sara nodded. "I respect their beliefs, but they're missing so much of life, and don't even know it."

"Mom, how do you think the opening went today?"

"Well, once the mayor quit talking about himself and his great achievements, it was terrific. That man sure is a windbag, isn't he? As a matter of fact, several folks near me completely ignored him after the first few minutes.

"When the two of you started talking, people began to listen again. I noticed how cheerful and attentive they became, especially the folks that brought their animals along. They were hanging on to every word you said. I think everybody was impressed with the young policeman, Mark, too."

Chantel and William both concurred, as they too had been moved by Mark's sincerity and his communication skills.

"They *loved* your singing, Chantel. I don't believe anyone was expecting that sort of treat. The clouds above looked like dozens of angels joining you in song. To me that's when everything really started coming together. It seemed as though the crowd was collectively sharing your vision. And then of course, darling Huck and Tabitha—what fun they had!"

William said, "Yeah, those are two terrific animals. They're great ambassadors for the sanctuary, aren't they? I really think they'll be very happy here and will welcome other animals as they come. Did you hear the beautiful tones after the two of them dropped off to sleep?"

The two women looked at him quizzically. Sara asked, "What tones?"

"Well, first I thought someone was playing one of those crystal singing bowls. These were deep tones reverberating all around, but seeming to come from the forest. Then the sound moved overhead to the middle of the meadow. Nobody else appeared to hear anything. Do you suppose the nature beings were intoning a blessing?"

Chantel smiled lovingly at her husband. "Sweetheart, that must have been exactly what it was, and how fortunate you are to have heard them!"

Thoughtfully, she continued, "Hmmm…maybe

when we concentrate so hard on one sense, it blocks out the others." Then after a pause: "I didn't hear anything, but when Huck and Tabitha were playing together, I noticed there was a companion with them. He was a gnome-like creature dressed in brown—looked like a little old man but was only the size of a small child. He had a big grin as he threw bright balls of energy for the animals to fetch. After a while, he raced with them to the edges of the property. It seemed he was enjoying the games just as much as the dog and cat were.

"And then there were the sparkles throughout the meadow—flitting points of light in rainbow hues. They would concentrate in one area, make a pattern in the grass, then disperse randomly for a few moments. Then they'd reappear in a different part of the meadow, making a different pattern. Reminded me of the tiny, winged nature beings that I used to see as a child, but these were so small it was impossible to tell anything about them except that they glowed with changing colors."

Sara interrupted. "Oh my goodness—I saw those too, but thought they were just dewdrops! There they were, right in front of me, and I didn't even realize they were moving around in changing patterns and colors!"

The three of them sat quietly with their individual memories. After a while William broke the silence. "It there a term for somehow just *knowing*, without specifically seeing or hearing?"

"Clairsentience maybe, or intuition?" suggested Chantel.

"Sure, either of those will do. I didn't hear or see it, but near the end of the dedication, I sensed strongly there were about a dozen tall slender columns ringing the meadow. They shimmered with gold, green and white light. My impression was that it was a dynamic structure built to protect and nurture the purpose of this place."

Sara nodded in agreement—the idea of protection for this nature sanctuary made perfect sense to her.

Chantel concurred: "That's almost exactly what I saw in my mind's eye—but to me it was a dozen shining angels. They were still, at full attention, and so slim they looked like columns of light. But when I mentally looked upward searching for some sort of roofing, I was surprised to see faces instead. They were in deep concentration, manipulating lines of light into a protective shell around the sanctuary."

There was a pounding on the back door. Sara jumped up to open it for Tom, who was holding two buckets overflowing with berries. She gasped, "Tom—what in the world happened to you? You look like something the cat dragged in!"

Tom, usually very meticulous about his appearance, was thoroughly disheveled. His trousers were muddy and torn, his shirt and face streaked with blood and grass stains; twigs and leaves were stuck in his hair. Despite this, he flashed a huge grin as he placed the brim-full buckets by the sink.

Chantel looked at him quizzically, "Are you all right, Dad? Did you get hurt on your hike?"

"I've never been better in my life! Just need to get cleaned up. I'll see you all in a little while." With that, he bounded out of the kitchen like a teenager instead of the sedate retiree he was.

After a few minutes he returned, looking his usual neat and tidy self. He chuckled, "I really looked a mess, didn't I? No wonder you were concerned that something happened to me. And as a matter of fact, something *did*. Want to hear about it?"

"Of course we do!" Sara answered, speaking for all of them.

"I had an *amazing* experience out there. There's no logical explanation for what happened, but…*everything's changed* now. It started out very ordinary. I was just wandering through the woods looking for berries. The bushes close to the trails had pretty well been picked, so I left the trail to see if the more remote areas would have better prospects.

"They sure did. I started finding more and more berries. Pretty soon the buckets were full, but I'd ended up way off course."

"Were you lost, Dad?" interrupted Chantel.

"Not quite… well, maybe. I'd never been in that part of the woods before, and there was lots of really thick undergrowth that I wasn't expecting…Yeah, I did get a little disoriented.

"OK, I'll admit it—I was lost. As I looked around trying to find my bearings again, I saw what looked like crumbling walls—the ruins of an old cabin. I began working my way toward it for a better view when suddenly there was no ground underneath my feet."

Chantel gasped and Sara cried out, "Tom!"

"You know how sometimes your mind goes into hyper-speed in emergencies? Everything flashes before you in no time? While I was still falling, I instantly realized that this was an old hand-dug well, so deep that that I wouldn't be able to get out by myself even if I didn't break both legs. I also knew that no one would be able to hear me and that there was no way to signal for help. All this happened in a flash.

"You know how you guys are always talking about a world beyond this one—colors beyond the ones we see, music that nobody else can hear, and the presence of other beings," Looking straight at William, he finished, "even communicating with animals?"

William nodded thoughtfully–they'd discussed that many times before, invariably agreeing to disagree on that topic.

"As you very well know, I've never believed in that sort of stuff—fairy tales like that are for kids, not for grown people. This is the real world: what I can see, hear, feel, touch, smell and taste. Certainly, if it's not logical and provable, it's not real."

"But," he continued after a long pause, "before I hit the bottom of the well, all of a sudden there were four strong arms securely around me. They lifted me up quickly (just as fast as I'd dropped down) and placed me back on the path a few feet away from the well bore. I spun around to thank my rescuers, but there was no one there—just a fresh clean scent almost like cedar. Funny, though, there's no cedar trees within miles of here!"

Sara and Chantel ran over and hugged him hard.

Tom chuckled. "After checking for broken bones or other injuries, I realized that not only was I safe and totally unharmed, but the buckets had been placed on the trail beside me, still full of berries—not one had fallen out! Being lifted from the well shaft was a huge miracle, but it was just as impossible to explain the buckets of unspilled berries with logic. It was such a perfect finishing touch that I couldn't keep from laughing out loud.

"Nonphysical heroes do exist, and are they ever strong! I'll never doubt the existence of otherworldly beings again. Don't know if they were Angels, fairies, or—what is it that the Hindus call them—devas, but whatever they were, they saved my life!"

He poured himself a glass of tea, pulled out a chair and joined them at the table. "So, dear family—I finally *get it*—everything you've said for years has been true. Now that I've experienced a touch of the *real* world, I can hardly wait to hear your impressions and insights about the sanctuary dedication this morning. How about you telling me what was really happening at Saints' Acres!"

Sara interrupted him. "Sure, honey, we'll be happy to tell you. First, though, how about some of those berries? William, if you'll help me wash them, and Chantel will get the bowls, spoons and cream, we're in for a real treat!"

The berries were ready in a flash. Everyone concentrated on eating the delicious goodies. As soon as the last bowl was empty, the family enthusiastically began to relate their experiences once again, this time with the added joy of being able to include Tom fully in the conversation.

CHANTEL'S SONG

Chapter 17
Middle Years at the Sanctuary

Chantel turned up the heat a bit: a series of late winter storms left a cold residue that seeped in despite their best efforts at insulating their old house, the one that used to belong to her parents. Once again, she remembered her Mom and Dad's elation when they announced that they were retiring to Mexico. "Chantel, it's going to be warm all year round!"

Across the room, William put on a jacket and headed to the mailbox outside. He soon returned, handing Chantel the envelopes. "Here's something from your folks."

"It's so sweet that they prefer writing letters the old-fashioned way. Even though it takes more thought and effort, each of those letters becomes a family treasure." After a few minutes of reading, she said, "Honey, do you remember years ago when Mom and Dad took a Spanish course, and how everyone in class called her 'Sarita' because she was so petite? Well, Mom writes that now not only is she 'Sarita,' but Dad has become 'Tomaro'—maybe because he always enjoys eating. How about that?"

"Hmm—Sarita and Tomaro—yes, those names fit them perfectly. Are they still liking their new home?"

"They're incredibly happy—you'd have to pry them loose with a crowbar to get them to move back here." She continued reading, then chuckled. "Speaking of crowbars, Mom writes that Dad went diving for abalone a few weeks ago. You remove them from the rocks with an 'abalone iron' that works just like a small crowbar. Dad succeeded in prying one loose, and Mom cleaned and prepared it. It was lots of work, but they both agreed that it was delicious."

She checked the week's calendar. "Honey, Joe's bringing some new OLC kids tomorrow. Do you have any special jobs for them?"

He grinned at her. "Always! How about, well, expanding the kennels, clearing the encroaching forest, or, oh yeah, fixing the leaky roof on the shop. Any one of those should be a good project, after they get started with mucking out the kennels and learning to care for the animals."

In the morning, Joe arrived at the sanctuary with Chip and Alex, two slouching, surly-looking boys. Their curiosity and fear were almost hidden under a huge show of bravado. Joe sat them down in the office, giving them an overview of the sanctuary, its history and its purpose. He followed this with very firm, clear specifics about what was expected of them, including rewards and consequences. Just as he finished this initial orientation,

Chantel and William entered the room. Joe stood up and introduced them.

"Dr. Farragut, Mrs. Farragut, I'd like you to meet Chip and Alex. They tell me they've had some experience in construction."

Chantel smiled a welcome at the boys, and William extended his hand, saying, "Good to meet you—looking forward to your help on some of the sanctuary projects." Alex reluctantly took the proffered hand and made eye contact for an instant. Chip kept his hands in his pockets, staring sullenly at the floor.

William continued, "I'm sure Joe has told you, but I need to make it crystal clear too—the whole purpose of this sanctuary is to create a safe, caring place for animals that otherwise would have no chance at all. *Everything* we do is for the animals. Remember that and you'll do fine here."

Joe took over. "C'mon, guys, let's get you set up: the dogs are waiting."

Everyone who came here to work was first trained in the basic needs of animal care Only after that was second nature to them would they branch off into their specialties or learn new skills.

During this slow and patient process, one specific animal might bond with one of the young men. When that happened, it was a joy to see—mutual help, mutual understanding—wordless communication. Having experienced it themselves, the animals intuitively understood the feelings of these abused or neglected youngsters.

Joe carefully explained how to clean the spacious kennels and the importance of basic sanitation procedures, then issued the equipment and supplies to do that. Although they tried to hide it, Joe saw their eyes widen and knew the boys were frightened of this large group of animals. Even the thought of letting dogs out of the kennel was terrifying. Joe could almost hear them thinking, "What if they gang up on me, maul me and rip me to shreds?"

Joe had worked with many kids like these. Given enough time, he had faith that they'd turn out OK. Still, the first few weeks were always tough.

❋❋❋

Chip, so surly and withdrawn when he first arrived at the sanctuary, had become a devoted protégée of William. Chip was an avid, receptive student—the boy not only took care of the animals' physical needs, but also learned to use his intuition as a way of developing a deeper understanding. By now he had become nearly as good as William in communicating with them wordlessly. Although Chip was skilled at caring for all the animals, he had a special aptitude for horses.

"What would we ever do without Joe and his OLCs?" William asked.

Chantel responded, "Can't even imagine the work and expense there'd be if they weren't here to maintain and improve the sanctuary. For me, though, even more than the physical help is seeing the transformation of the kids in this atmosphere. It's magic!"

Reaching to take William's hand, she continued, "And you, sweetheart—your internship program is incredible! So many young vets have been through here: you've taught them all so patiently. From the hands-on experience of working with abused animals, to specialized surgical procedures, to learning the intuitive healing techniques you use so wisely, each one leaves with some aspect of your gifted work. And now two of them have decided to stay here working with you permanently—wow!"

William smiled lovingly at her. "Yes, they're terrific docs and I'd be comfortable leaving the sanctuary in their hands one day.

"How blessed we've been through this life. What a gift to be permitted to share it with you, sweet Chantel of the lovely voice! I'll love you always."

"And I will always love you," she replied. "If this were a story we were reading, we'd say it's far too Pollyanna-ish to be true—yet here we are."

They sat in quiet thanksgiving for a few moments more, then began their daily activities. Chantel drove to town to teach her singing students, and William headed to the barn to check on the most recent equine admission, a mare that had had been severely traumatized by beatings that left her body covered with scars and bruises. The fearful, bewildered, angry horse lashed out at all humans, and so far, no one had been able to get near her, much less ride her. The animal had been sent to the sanctuary as a last resort.

One of the staff had named her "Beauty." Very calmly and gently, speaking in a soothing voice and sending her waves of peace, William gradually approached Beauty. After perhaps half an hour he ever so slowly reached out to touch her. She shuddered but didn't move away. William continued to send her energies of calmness and peace as he began moving his hand along her body, feeling the spots of tensions and pain. At each one of these, he would pause, his fingers soothing the stresses. He felt Beauty's anger, her bafflement and her fear as she sent him images of the cruelty she'd borne for so long. William murmured, "Everything's going to be all right, Beauty. No one's going to hurt you. You're safe here."

After several days of this healing ritual, she became relaxed and trusting enough that she gladly followed William outside. After a few more days, she allowed him on her back. William had long ago found that riding bareback was the best way to become in tune with a horse and aware of its needs. He never used a saddle or reins when riding, believing that those devices interfered with two-way communication between horse and rider. He wanted to be a partner, not a dominant master of the animal. He let her lead the way. She cantered across the meadow and then followed a path into the surrounding woods.

After a mile or so, William patted her and said, "Beauty, it's time to go back now. There's other work to be done." She understood his intent, if not his words, and obligingly returned to the barn. William dismounted, saying "thank you" to the mare as he gave her a final pat. Proceeding to his full schedule of the day's assignments, he made a mental note: make sure to ride Beauty every morning to continue gaining her trust.

Over the next few months, William and Beauty had developed a well-established morning routine. This morning, as usual, he entered the barn, talked to her soothingly while checking her now-healed bruises, then led her outside and got on her back for their morning ride. This was a special time for them both: Beauty loved having William on her back as they roamed through the woods. William communicated with Beauty and also took this special time in nature to visualize the day ahead.

After a half hour or so they were both refreshed. Returning, they crossed the meadow, making their way through the sun-warmed glacial boulders, when suddenly a rattlesnake appeared in the path. The horse reared instinctively. With no time to react, William was thrown onto the rocks, hitting his head on a boulder.

He was unable to move or call out: searing pain raced throughout his body. Then—it was gone as though it had never existed. Now there was only light, glorious light, growing ever brighter. He heard a resonant, loving yet firm voice saying, "It's time to return to your true Home, William—come now!" The light expanded even more, and he was lifted within it. As he rose, he looked back to see his body crumpled like a rag doll in the meadow. He sent it a 'thank you' for serving him so well for his life on earth, at the same time realizing that this body was no more *him* than a pile of discarded clothing would be. He had just an instant to send thoughts of peace to Beauty, then experienced his whole being merging into a oneness of infinite Light and Love beyond description.

※ ※ ※

Later that morning, Chip glanced from his work assignment and saw the mare standing in the meadow, her head down and body not moving. Realizing that this was very unusual behavior for Beauty, he hurried out to the meadow to see what was going on. As Chip came up, the horse remained stock still, watching over and protecting William's body. Nearby lay the hoof-mangled remains of a rattlesnake.

On discovering William, Chip was inconsolable. "If only I'd been there, I could have helped! The only person who ever understood me is gone! I should have been there!"

Shattered, he guided Beauty back into the barn, and rushed to bring the sad news to Chantel. He performed his tasks like an automaton, agonizing about the loss of William. His grief and despair lasted for weeks.

Then one morning he felt a hand firmly clasping his shoulder and heard William's voice saying: "Don't grieve for me, Chip—I'm fine, and *more alive than ever.* Your gift of understanding animals will help you through this. Always remember to keep your heart open to the highest good."

This revelation totally changed Chip. Those words resounded throughout his entire being. Then and there he vowed to do the best he could, forever, to honor William and to bless the animals under his care. The only one he shared this experience with was Beauty. She whinnied softly in response to his words as he took her for her morning ride. From that moment on, Chip and Beauty had an unbreakable bond.

The entire staff at the sanctuary mourned William's death. In their individual ways, they grieved, they despaired, they doubted, they didn't see how the sanctuary could continue. But gradually they were strengthened in an awareness that the mission of the sanctuary was unchanged, and that each of them would be responsible for part of its realization. They found ways to transmute their grief into a resolve to continue William's legacy. They knew that no one person could take William's place, but collectively all of them could, and would, do their utmost for the animals.

Chantel remained steadfastly filled with faith, a beacon of light in the surrounding darkness. Her grief at the loss of William from this life was deep, yet permeated with gratitude for the wonderful years they'd shared together. A few days before his passing, he had confided in her that he'd been diagnosed with inoperable cancer of a particularly aggressive type and would have only weeks or months to live. They had prayed together about this just before William left on his fateful horseback ride. In a way, this was an answer to prayer: a deliverance from what would have been a time of agonizing pain.

Chantel knew without a doubt that William was more alive than ever now. She could no longer see him but sensed his presence often. She knew too, that her Guardian Angel was constantly at her side, strengthening her with love and courage for the time ahead.

❈ ❈ ❈

William's Memorial service was held a month later, in the meadow of the sanctuary. Nearly the whole town turned out, plus many of Joe's former OLC kids, and dozens of people from all over the country who had been inspired by their time at the sanctuary with William. Some of them were veterinarians, others ran animal shelters or animal rescue institutions, still others had become teachers. Every one of them had learned invaluable lessons from William.

During the deeply moving service, Chantel saw two different types of Angels ringing the meadow, standing at full attention to honor William. They sent forth a special benediction to all those present, including the animals. At the very end, she again heard the poignant strains of *"Hello, Hello, Hello, My Love"* sung by the nature beings, exactly as she remembered first hearing it so many years ago on the mountaintop. As the music ended, just for an instant she saw William, glowing with light. Behind him were throngs of beings joyfully welcoming him home. The light within and around him became so bright she had to close her eyes. When she opened them again, he was gone.

Smiling through her tears, she breathed, "Thank you, dearest God. This moment is a treasure that will live in my heart forever. And thank you, sweetheart—until we meet again!"

Chapter 18
FULL CIRCLE

Chantel addressed the board of the Francis Blaise Martin Foundation and Sanctuary for the last time. "It's miraculous how the Sanctuary's grown, not only in size but in scope of services offered for the animals. For so many years it was our dream—William's and mine—and now it's not only a reality but has become an integral part of the community. It's as though it has always been here!

"It's hard to step down from the board now, but the time has come to pass on the torch. Please know how much I appreciate the work that every one of you has done and is doing to preserve the Sanctuary, to help the animals, and to give troubled youths another chance. As you know, you hold in your hands a sacred trust—to continue its mission."

The board president responded: "This is all due to the vision of both you and William. Without that, none of this would have happened. On behalf of the board, the staff, the animals over the years, and the community, we thank you."

Smiling graciously, Chantel moved to her seat. Over these past years, her body had developed several problems including a heart condition and severe arthritis, but her mind remained clear, positive and upbeat. Although her hair was now fully white and wrinkles crosshatched her face, her blue eyes still sparkled, and her smile was as bright as ever.

The board began discussing procedural items, and Chantel's thoughts shifted to her upcoming activities. She still taught several gifted singing students, all showing promise for a musical career. Three of them had become especially close to her. They would often stay a while with her after class, sharing tea along with lively discussions about personal beliefs and experiences. During such a conversation recently, she had mentioned one of her own treasured nature-oriented singing meditations. She'd called this one her "tree-listening, tree-singing" practice.

Their eyes got wide. "Could you teach us how to do that?"

She looked at them intently, determined that their interest was genuine, and inwardly sensed their readiness for this step. They'd agreed to meet at Chantel's home early the following Saturday, before the sun would have had time to melt the nighttime frost.

Saturday dawned crisp and cold. The young singers arrived at 7 a.m., wrapped in heavy parkas and scarves. Chantel joined them, carrying a walking stick but wearing only indoor clothing. The girls gasped and immediately offered her their coats. Chantel's response was, "Thank you for offering, but I won't need a coat."

She continued with a smile, "Good job, though! You've all passed your first test of the day—being willing to give something you need to someone else."

As they approached the bridge, the one that Chantel's father and William had built so long ago, Chantel shared the story of its creation. They then crossed the meadow and entered the woods on an easy-to-miss path that Chantel obviously knew well. She guided her students through the dense forest for perhaps half a mile. Rounding a corner, the path suddenly opened to a sunlit clearing ringed by majestic trees. Chantel had the girls move toward its center. Once they were there in a ring, she directed them in the deep breathing exercises they'd learned in singing classes—to bring themselves also to centeredness.

After that, she had them each rotate individually in a full circle, clockwise, very slowly. Then Chantel asked them to describe what they observed. As they shared their impressions, she nodded, giving them encouraging feedback.

After a moment, Chantel said, "This time turn in the other direction, and become more fully aware of the scents, the sounds, the sights, the feel of your surroundings. Each time you rotate, alternate your direction." As before, she had them share their observations, occasionally offering a few words of wise counsel. After they responded this time, she had them turn yet again, searching even deeper. This time she suggested that they emphasize a different sense than they had previously used. The next time she asked them to add deep, peaceful breathing to their slow circling. With each repeated cycle, the girls responded more calmly, thoughtfully and creatively.

Finally, she asked each of them to be receptively alert for a feeling, a hint, or a subtle guidance—to aid in selecting a specific tree that seemed most special to them. She instructed the students: "For now, this will be 'your' tree. As you walk toward it, imagine a great and beautiful entity inhabiting this tree, if you wish. Acknowledge and send a tone of love to the tree: a single note from your heart. Stand with your arms around its trunk. Sing your tone for three long breaths. Then, still with your arms around it, and maintaining total silence, continue to send your tree love. Visualize a bridge of harmony being created between the two of you. Open yourself completely to the tree; feeling what it feels…trusting its message. Listen for its pulse of life. Patiently wait, stilling and clearing your mind, so that you can hear its song. Slowly and softly, when the time is right, join with the tree in singing: first in unison, then in harmony. When your song has blended and is finished, be sure to thank your co-singer tree."

The girls looked quizzically at her; not entirely sure she was serious. She gazed steadily back at them with a slight nod, indicating they were to do this. Within a few minutes, each of them had found her own tree and begun the exercise. The clearing was still, except for the occasional song of a bird. Then after several minutes, one girl began singing very softly. The next soon joined in with her own unique melody that somehow formed a counterpart to the other one. Finally, the last voice emerged. Although each girl heard only her own tree and her own voice, in a private cocoon of communion, the clearing was awash in music.

Chantel listened with delight. She heard not only the three human singers and the tones of their trees, but the grand harmony of the entire forest surrounding them.

When their musical meditation ended, the girls returned to the boulder where Chantel was sitting. She asked with a grin, "Did you notice anything different about the temperature?" The girls looked at her, astonished at this very prosaic question, then burst out laughing. Although barely aware of it at the time, each of them had removed their parkas and gloves when they were communicating with their tree, basking in its warmth, sharing its love. Chantel added, "That's why I never need a coat in the meadow. Even though the frost may still be here, the warmth of love from the trees is always present."

Returning to the meadow, they were greeted by a throng of eager and happy animals enjoying their first romp of the day. The girls spent a few minutes greeting them affectionately before going their separate ways. Chantel returned to her home and made a cup of tea. Sipping it in her recliner, she silently reflected: "It's been a good life, and a long one, dear Lord. I thank you for all your gifts, your blessings, and the experiences in growth you've given me. But now I'm tired and often in pain: this body is wearing out. When the tasks you've assigned are done—well, whenever you wish to set me free, Lord, I'm ready."

Her head nodded as she drifted off to sleep. Then, with an electrical shock of joy, she emerged into a world of pure light. Celestial tones rang all around her: strains of the song she'd first heard so long ago, but incredibly more glorious than she'd ever imagined it could be. Shining beings surrounded her, beaming waves of love to her. As she looked around, she saw Tomaro, sweet little Sarita, and vast numbers of long-passed dear friends, teachers, relatives, Angel companions. When she could speak, she thanked them all with a grace-filled, thankful heart.

Searching the group to find the one she'd missed the most, Chantel quickly found William—strong, young and glowing—awaiting her. He wrapped her in his arms, lifted her and spun her around just as he had those many years ago in the meadow—"Welcome Home, dear heart—welcome Home!"

Made in the USA
Columbia, SC
29 June 2021